# IT'S A GRIMM LIFE

edited by James S. Austin

Tacitus Publishing
PO Box 2466
Largo, FL 33779

*It's a Grimm Life*

Edited by James S. Austin

Published by Tacitus Publishing

www.tacituspublishing.com

© 2015  Tacitus Publishing.  All Rights Reserved

ISBN:  978-0-9848612-0-0


Cover art by James S. Austin
Illustrations by James S. Austin

## Acknowledgments

When embracing a project that depends on the talents of many, there is much thanks to go around. First, thank you to Toby LeCrone and Ruth L. Austin for their technical expertise. Their hours of scrutiny cannot go unrecognized. A huge thank you to all the contributing authors and those that took the time to submit. They are the lifeblood that must continue to be pumped into this new age of publishing.

A special thanks needs to go out to all those who indirectly supported this Grimm project, to include Michael Cardamone, Heather Loomis, Michael Kelleher, and Gary Przybyla. Those that surround us make us stronger.

# Table of Contents

# Forward

Cultures throughout the world have folktales that carry warnings hidden within. They illustrate what could happen if we surrender to our brutish nature. The first accounts can be found in the oral traditions of a people, passed from generation to generation, before pen touched paper. One of the most notable collections to be later recorded is *Kinder- und Hausmärchen*, translating to 'Children's and Household Tales', published by Jacob and Wilhelm Grimm in 1812. The impact this project has had on all parts of our lives, and throughout the world, is nearly incomprehensible.

*It's a Grimm Life* is a tribute to these resounding folktales from the past, placing them in a modern setting. Each story is germinated from a Grimm seed, embracing the darker side of humanity and the world that we know to exist in the shadows, just out of sight.

Darker than dark, grimmer than Grimm
What foul temptations lie within?

Unlike the tales you read as a child
There's nothing here for the meek and mild

You can't be squeamish where souls are sold,
And bargains are made in pursuit of fool's gold

Jealousy, revenge are ill-advised friends
In pacts with the devil as the means to an end

Dark paths you'll trudge, your soul now damned
Confront your debts, payment on demand

You'll pay the piper or the wicked witch
Who own the odds when your life's a bitch

Yes, you, you feel it! You've got the itch
A greed, a lust to be powerful and rich

Now here at my door you're all alone
Nervous, naked as the dead man's bones

Like the others you fret, yet you're willingly led
When my sly incantations start in your head

Relax, resign, come on in
Too late, you're mine, our stories begin


- by Steve Keteltas

WHO'S AFRAID?

by Carl Barker

Tennessee is a wonderful place during the summer months; a rich palette of colours mixing vivid Catawba pinks with the rolling purples of Mount Conte.  A pity then, that Phillip travelled her roads in the midst of January, a hoar-frost coating his stubble as a reminder.  Spindly trees formed a funeral procession alongside the highway he walked, their heads bowed heavy with snow.  Why was it that the simplest memories faded, yet the most terrifying remained?

He recalled that day in Tal Afar well enough: how he'd saved Milo Peeg from an insurgent grenade and come to realise that there was such a thing as a choice.  That day had been the beginning of a conflict between his mind and his body, to prevent himself from ever losing control again.

## It's a Grimm Life

The directions from Coker Creek had been simple—follow the road up the mountain till you can't feel your feet—but that point had already passed and still he trudged upwards, ignoring his growing fatigue. Had there even been a time when he hadn't been tired? Tired of war, tired of killing, tired of listening to the sound of men die for a flag? Phillip's dusty boots trod the dirt like a metronome, but the fatigue was controllable, easy enough to block out with his training. They were good like that, the Army, teaching you to ignore things like fatigue, and pain, and emotion.

The road wove through the conifers like a tarmac-skinned snake, headed towards a trio of oversized mansions huddled conspiratorially at the top the mountain: his intended destination. A solitary logging truck rumbled by, flinging oil-freckled snow, and Phillip spat out a bit of dirt, pulling the threads of his meagre coat tighter. He'd been sleeping rough for over a week again, finding shelter wherever he could, but as the month drew to a close, he needed a roof over his head before the moon became full.

Wind yanked the strands of his beard like an irate coachman, the cold so intense that no amount of warm breath could depose it. Determined to block out the pain, he stuffed frozen hands into his jacket and remembered a line from his father—that cold warriors had no fear of winter. Phillip's father had said a lot of things like that; occasional sound-bites designed to summarize the bleak truths of the world. It was how he'd come to terms with the war and the atrocities he'd committed. Phillip's father had come home a monster, in more ways than one.

Beneath his shirt, Phillip wore his father's Special Service Medal, bequeathed to him on the condition that he would forever keep it safe. Phillip thought of it as the last link between them (other than blood) and wore it always, on a chain round his neck. The eight pointed star dug into his skin, causing unintended discomfort, much as his father's words had once done.

\* \* \* \* \*

He reached the first mansion late in the day—a thoroughly southern affair, wooden, antebellum and grand. It reeked of power and greed. Scaling locked metal gates, he made his way up the driveway, enjoying the feel of loose gravel beneath his feet after hours of tarmac. The bell-pull was a solid black rod which summoned a well-tailored manservant to the door.

"May I help you, sir?" he enquired.

"I'm looking for somebody," Phillip grunted, unaccustomed to manners.

The elderly butler eyed him with a frown, gaze roaming over Phillip's shabby attire.

"I should say that you have found someone, sir."

"No, that's not quite what I meant. I'm looking for someone in particular. A guy I served with in Iraq. His name's Milo Peeg."

The butler stiffened.

"Won't you come in, sir?" he beckoned. "I'll announce your arrival."

Phillip stepped into an elaborate hallway and followed the butler through several much larger rooms to an indoor swimming pool. He observed the butler bent over a figure seated in the far corner, but could see only a highly polished pair of loafers. The butler moved aside, revealing an overtly fat man in a white linen suit. The fastidiousness of his attire was offset by a crudely deformed nose, which turned up slightly at one end and was sunk into his face, the cartilage forming a rough circle of flesh, upon which perched a pair of sunglasses. Getting up from his seat, the man slowly waddled over to greet him.

"I'm sorry," he began, tucking his newspaper snugly under one arm. "I don't believe I've had the pleasure?"

Phillip eyed the man's familiar hereditary disfigurement.

"My name's William Peeg," his host tried again, offering a well manicured hand. "And you would be?"

Phillip tried to discern something of his host from this initial reaction, but there was a darkness about the man that seemed to permanently shroud him, the dark glasses forming a perfect contrast to the white of his suit.

"Phillip Marshall," he answered.

Peeg raised an eyebrow.

"And what exactly can I do for you, Mr. Marshall?"

Peeg's smile was that of a crocodile, toothsome and threatening, as though he'd like nothing more than to drag Phillip down into murky dark water and starve him of air.

"I'm looking for somebody."

"Hmm, I see," replied Peeg, consulting his pocket watch. "Might I offer you a Mint Julep?"

Phillip searched through his pockets and pulled out a crumpled Polaroid.

"I served with him in Iraq."

"My goodness, Mr Marshall, you do get around," Peeg fawned. "Though I'm not sure that..."

His voice trailed off at the sight of the photo.

14

"His name's Milo Peeg," Phillip reiterated, locking eyes with his host. "I'm guessing that just maybe you know him?"

The colour drained from Peeg's face, turning the skin round his nose a deep shade of crimson.

"I'm afraid not," he sputtered, clearly perturbed. "Maxwell, would you be so good as to show this gentleman out? It seems that he and I have concluded our business."

The butler glided obediently forward but Phillip remained a moment, watching as Peeg tottered over to a nearby drinks cabinet and poured himself a generous measure of bourbon, downing the glass in one gulp with a trembling hand. Phillip reluctantly returned the photograph to his pocket and followed the butler out.

* * * * *

Once back outside the gate, Phillip stood bewildered in the cold, ejected from the house like a bad case of gas. The recognition when Peeg had seen Milo's picture was obvious, but Phillip was at a loss to explain why the man would claim not to know someone to whom he was almost certainly related. An uncle, or more likely a brother, judging by age.

The proper name for the deformity was Von Recklinghausen disease. Back in the unit, Milo had jokingly referred to it as his Hapsburg Lip, on account of it being hereditary. Phillip's own condition meant the two of them had bonded when they bunked together in the barracks. Milo's family had made their money in gold, his father leaving his entire fortune to his eldest son when he died, but Milo had preferred to sign up and do his

15

bit for his country, despite his affliction. Phillip had watched him stride through the ranks, head held high in defiance, and learnt that courage was not something they pinned to your chest. It came from inside.

The next mansion was larger than the first, set back from the road in a thick copse of trees. Barbed wire fences and security cameras gave the stench of new money, as did the overtly tattooed oak gate. In the garden beyond he could hear a deep, thrumming bass. Staying out of sight of the cameras, he mounted the gate and followed the sound to an enormous straw cabana behind the main house. Topped by a domed roof of woven grass, it resembled a Samoan hut. From within came a harrowing dirge of noise, as someone fumbled their way badly through the chorus of 'Bad Moon Rising' on an electric guitar. As Phillip drew near, the music abruptly stopped and a tubby runt in a Megadeth T-shirt emerged. Jeans riddled with designer holes, he wore a solid gold chain round his neck bearing the word 'Jiggs' in an elaborate script. Shading his eyes against the sudden daylight, the youth squinted at Phillip through tinted John Lennon glasses.

"And just who the hell is you, like?"

His accent was an odd mixture of colloquialisms, as though the kid might have moved round, but to Phillip, who had travelled extensively, it was a gross imitation, a vain attempt by the boy to mimic the legendary rockers which he so clearly worshipped.

"Ere, I'm talking to you, mate," Jiggs demanded, glasses wobbling atop a familiar deformity. "You're clearly not from the label, so what's the dish?"

Phillip held up his photograph.

"You know this guy? He's a friend of mine."

The kid inspected the picture, before hocking up a thick wad of phlegm.

"Piss off," he spat.

Phillip's hands were round the kid's throat in seconds, pushing his head back on that stumpy white neck.

"Now," Phillip instructed, struggling to rein in his temper. "I'm going to ask you again."

The kid's eyes bulged round the bulb of his nose, giving Phillip the sudden urge to thrust an apple into his mouth.

"His name's Milo," the kid gurgled. "He's my older brother."

"Tell me something I don't know," Phillip said, constricting his grasp.

"He's... dead" the youth squealed, his rotund face going purple.

Phillip released him and the kid slid to the floor. Reaching into his pocket, Jiggs withdrew a small buzzer and thumbed the main button, summoning two heavily-muscled bodyguards from inside the house. Clad in identical pin-stripe suits, they lumbered purposefully across the lawn to stand at either side of their boss.

"Yeah, that's right, Bubba," Jiggs sneered as he clambered back to his feet. "Milo's been dead and gone these last five years or more, eaten up by cancer till he weren't more than a husk."

A strange glee lit the kid's eyes.

"So if you want to catch up with your buddy, you best be heading down to Coker Creek Cemetery."

The photograph slid from Phillip's hand, lost to the wind.

"This here is Maurice," announced the kid, tapping the chest of the nearest gorilla. "And this here is Leslie. They're my guardian angels, and it's their job to take out the trash."

Phillip wasn't listening, his thoughts centred on Milo. It seemed that saving him from that grenade had just postponed the inevitable. Perhaps Phillip's father had been right when he said a man could never escape his destiny.

"Boys," the kid frothed. "Perhaps you'd like to throw my visitor out on his ear?"

The two bodyguards darted forward and began manhandling Phillip across the front lawn, ripping his jacket as they dragged him back out into the street. Pausing to readjust his tie, the larger of the men bestowed an insipid grin.

"Mr Peeg doesn't like to be disturbed when he's making his music, so clear off, chump."

"Isn't Leslie a girl's name?" Phillip needled, wiping blood from his lip.

The bodyguard grunted once before slamming the gate.

With the cold nipping at his ankles, Phillip stared dejectedly out across the valley. Slinging his duffel bag over one shoulder, he continued his climb up the road.

* * * * *

Deep inside the Peeg ancestral home, a leather armchair sat before a roaring hearth. Outside the thick, castle-like walls, a howling wind lapped at the stonework like a hungry dog, its whine reduced to a curtailed whisper

In one hand, Elmer Peeg held a Cuban cigar, its tip a smouldering ember.  In the other, he grasped a porcelain phone, listening as his younger brothers, William and Jethro, took turns in explaining how they'd just been interrogated by some wandering vagrant.

William, always the brighter and more promising of the two, was informing him that the stranger was an acquaintance of their late brother and seemed determined to locate him, when Elmer cut him off mid-sentence.

"What exactly did you tell him, William?"

"Nothing, brother, I swear it ..."

Elmer sensed a 'but' and ground his cigar irritably into his ashtray.

"…though I'm afraid Jiggs may have done something rather foolish."

Elmer snorted, having expected as much.  Tossing the extinguished cigar into the fire, he leant forward over his copious girth.

"The cemetery?" he grunted, displacing stray ash from his waistcoat.  "Why would he go and say a fool thing like that?"

There was a momentary pause, during which Jethro could be heard mumbling incoherently in the background.

"Cancer!" Elmer exclaimed in response to his answer.  "If there's any cancer in this family, then it's the one in that fool's addled brain.  And what pray, does young Jethro think will happen if our inquisitive visitor elects to go down to the cemetery and investigate further?"

Another bout of muffled discourse followed, during which Elmer wearily rubbed his temples, wishing he'd been born an only child.

"He says he doesn't know, brother," came William's nervous reply.

"That boy doesn't know much of anything," snorted Elmer. "I'll tell you what's going to happen, William. You're going to let me handle this infernal mess, with my usual zeal and innate flare for creativity."

There was a slightly strangled sound on the other end of the phone and Elmer hung up in disgust.

Picking furiously at his snout, he dislodged a small morsel of food, flicking the snotty piece of fat into the heart of the fire, where it sizzled and popped. Reaching for the phone again, Elmer began dialling a more useful number.

\* \* \* \* \*

Sheriff Archibald Beazel was not having a good day. Having woken up with a hangover just after twelve, he had made his way down to the station to find that Dougie Wilson had driven his truck into a pylon and shorted out half the town's power. The fact that he had been well over the legal limit came as no real surprise, and having provided Dougie with the usual jailhouse bed and board for the night, Beazel had retired to his office, determined to investigate nothing else except a twelve-year Scotch. When Elmer Peeg called a little after six, he had barely finished his first glass and, reluctantly stowing the bottle back into his drawer, he'd headed out to his cruiser muttering something about there being no rest for the wicked.

Despite his position of authority, Beazel still felt like an impostor in Coker Creek. Every day he half-expected someone to discover the pact he'd made with the town Devil and demand his resignation forthwith. The Devil was waiting for him now, up there in his castle, tugging Archie's strings between chubby, oversized fingers. Beazel hated the fact that he was in Elmer Peeg's pocket, but the offer had been too good to turn down; a position of respect amongst the townsfolk, a full clearing of his gambling debts and a licence to carry a gun. Despite his misgivings, Archie had done what any self-respecting chancer would have done in his place and said yes to the deal. The problem was that each day he spent wearing this badge was another day closer to someone discovering his secret. He knew now that he should have said no to the pact, but he had been too weak a man. As the dark shadow of his taskmaster's abode came into view, Beazel wondered whether he'd ever had any choice in the matter.

\* \* \* \* \*

Phillip heard the engine long before the headlights pierced the gloom surrounding the towering gatehouse. He'd reached the last mansion just before dusk, stopped in his tracks by the sheer size of the place. This, he realised, was the magnificent ancestral home which Milo had so often spoken of. A veritable fortress guarding a treasure trove of family secrets, and the place which Phillip felt sure held the answers to his numerous questions.

The lights of the police cruiser cast his silhouette against the high stone walls as a grey-haired beanpole of a man climbed warily out of the car.

"Something I can help you with, son?"

Phillip observed the way that the man's left hand rested nervously on the butt of his gun.

"You got a tongue in that head, boy?"

The lawman stood there watching him intently, waiting for some response.

"I suppose you know that we got laws about 'loitering with intent' in this county?"

Phillip evaluated the Sheriff's holstered firearm as he approached - a Smith & Wesson .40 automatic by the shape of it, fifteen in the clip with one in the chamber - plenty of stopping power and big enough to put a couple of decent size holes in a man.

"It's a free country," he replied, meeting the steady gaze.

"That it is, son" the Sheriff said with a smirk. "But when I see a guy with less than two cents to his name loitering outside the home of Coker Creek's wealthiest citizen, I get to thinking maybe he's up to no good."

"Is it against the law to ask people questions?" Phillip asked tersely, sliding both hands behind his back, in an attempt to obscure the clench of his fists.

It was the wrong move, and Beazel's pistol was out of its holster in seconds.

"No it ain't," he continued. "But seeing as harassment and trespassing are, I figure we'll be taking a little ride down to the station."

Deciding that starting a fight with the law in this town was probably not the best strategy, Phillip meekly allowed himself to be handcuffed and bundled into the back of the cruiser. Letting out a long sigh, he watched the Sheriff re-holster his weapon and glance up at the house, an uneasy compliance in his eyes. Phillip began to get a sense of how things worked in this town.

\* \* \* \* \*

"What's this one in for then, Sheriff?" asked the pimpled desk sergeant as they entered the Station.

"Vagrancy..." replied Beazel in a tired voice, his thoughts straying back to that Scotch.

"...and disturbing the peace."

Phillip glared at him, knowing full well that to argue was useless.

The sound of the deputy's pen scratching across the charge sheet was like pins in his head and he grimaced, a low rumbling beginning way down in his gut. Phillip found himself breaking into a cold sweat.

A second deputy, much larger than the first, stepped through the rear doors with an Alsatian padding obediently along at his heels. Upon seeing Phillip, the dog began growling, pulling frantically against the thick leash that held it. Cuffing the dog sharply across the nose, the deputy shut it away in one of the side offices before sagging onto the corner of a nearby desk.

"Looks like Attila don't like you much" he chuckled. "You'd best be hoping I don't let him come down to the cells tonight for a visit."

Phillip barely heard him, a loud buzzing filling his head. Surrounded by the three men, he felt like a wild animal caught in a trap.

"Hey," yelled the larger deputy. "I'm talking to you, boy."

Pulling out the baton at his side, the deputy leant forward and tapped one end firmly against Phillip's chest with a clink.

"Well, well," smiled the deputy. "What do we have hidden under here?"

Phillip flinched as the man pulled out the medal.

23

"What you got there, Floyd?" asked the kid at the desk.

"R-V-N Special Service Medal," read Floyd, tearing it loose. "What's that, Vietnam?"

He shoved Phillip back with the ball of his hand.

"You some kind of war hero?" he asked mockingly.

Phillip eyed the baton, imagining what it would feel like to ram it down Floyd's throat. He couldn't lose control. Not now. Not here. Not again.

"Cool it, Floyd," Beazel called from his office. "Our friend there's not old enough to have served over there. It's probably just an heirloom or something."

The Sheriff emerged from his office with a half-full glass in his hand. Behind him, on the wall, Phillip spied a Remington rifle.

"Nah, I reckon he stole it," Floyd argued, "probably lifted it from some veteran's home, along with the poor bastard's life-savings."

Phillip's head snapped round at the accusation.

"That's as maybe," Beazel countered. "But until we get him before Judge Mayhew tomorrow morning and pull his record, I ain't jumping to conclusions."

Retrieving the cell keys from a nearby hook, he steered Phillip towards the rear of the station.

"Come on, son, let's get you a bed for the night."

\* \* \* \* \*

Three tiny cells comprised the whole of the station's miniscule jail. The first cell was empty, but in the second, a middle-aged man lay flat-out on a cot, snoring loudly.

Beazel opened up the third cell and pushed Phillip briskly inside, motioning for him to hold his hands up to the bars whilst he unlocked the cuffs. The cell's only window was barred and the skylight far too high to reach. A pale glow emanated from above as the wind scattered the last of the clouds.

Panicking, Phillip reached out for the Sheriff.

"Please," he begged. "You can't put me in here."

Beazel calmly backed out of reach.

"Sorry friend," he replied. "You're here for the night."

Phillip's stomach cramped painfully, a familiar sensation of bodily dislocation beginning in his lower back.

"You don't understand. I can't stay in here, it's not safe," he pleaded.

Beazel grinned.

"What, you mean old Dougie there? Why, he ain't no trouble."

The Sheriff planted a well-aimed kick at the bars of the next cell, waking its resident rudely from slumber.

"Please Sheriff," Phillip tried one last time. "I can't be responsible for what happens if you leave me in here."

Beazel stepped up to the bars, eyeballing his house guest.

"Sometimes", he replied solemnly. "A man ain't got no more choices in life."

Securing the bunch of keys to a ring on his belt, he plodded slowly back to his office, locking the main door to the cellblock behind him.

With his anxiety rising, Phillip retreated back from the moonlight and collapsed alongside the bed, pulling himself into a tight ball as he stared up at the skylight. Sweat racked his body from head to toe, soaking through his clothes and pooling in the soles of his shoes.

In the next cell, Dougie sat up in drunken bewilderment and stared at his surroundings.

"Choice," Phillip whispered. "There has to be choice."

The words were familiar, muttered on nights just like this one. Sometimes he faltered and gave in to it, but more often than not he refused to surrender, holding the animal back till the dawn came. This time though, the only words in his head were those of that cursed runt, Jiggs:

'He's dead, eaten up by cancer. No more than a husk.'

Hopelessness descended over Phillip like fog, His father was right. When he'd been set loose in that faraway jungle, he'd known full well what Phillip was, and what his boy might become.

"No," Phillip whimpered, head clutched in his hands. "Milo can't be dead."

"What's that you say?" coughed the wino, wiping two bloodshot eyes.

Phillip glanced over at him.

"I couldn't save him," he sobbed. "I took that grenade for Milo, but I couldn't save him from cancer."

"Cancer?" Dougie Wilson spat. "What the hell you babbling about? Milo Peeg died from a gunshot wound, out in them woods."

As Phillip stared, the first spasm came, wrenching his body in three different directions at once. Falling to the floor, he let out a low moan and crawled over towards the neighbouring cell.

"What ... do you ... mean?" he begged between long panting breaths.

"They said he was out walking at dusk," Dougie grumbled, staggering over to the bucket in the corner and fumbling with his fly, his back towards Phillip. "Got mistaken for deer by a hunter—don't believe a word of it, myself".

"If you ask me," Dougie finished. "I reckon somebody had it in for that boy."

Phillip's body rocked with a second spasm and he jerked away from the bars. Grabbing at his chest, he let out a pained shriek as a large rip appeared down the back of his jacket, the bones of his spine swelling out like a worm.

Peering round, Dougie tripped over his own feet and fell in a heap on the floor, staring open-mouthed at Phillip with his dick still clutched in his hand.

"Jesus H Christ!" he screamed, back-pedalling away.

Hair erupted from Phillip's flesh and began to engulf his body. The line of his jaw stretched forwards and down into an elongated snout and he let out an unearthly howl between sharp canine teeth.

Through in the main office, the desk sergeant came barrelling round his desk with the cell keys in hand.

"God damn it, Floyd" he grumbled. "How many times have I told you not to let that dog in the cells?"

Unlocking the rear door, he noticed Floyd emerge from the kitchen, Attila skulking sheepishly between his oversized legs. Catching sight of the dog, the deputy frowned in confusion and tugged open the door to the cells, coming face to face with something that looked like it might have once been a man, but had now forgotten itself.

27

## It's a Grimm Life

The thing that was Phillip took hold of the deputy's skull between clawed hands and wrenched the kid's head from his body like the top from a doll, spraying Floyd's face with a fine mist of blood. The giant reached for his baton but only had time for one brief scream before Phillip raked his flesh with oversized talons, cutting him to the bone, falling onto the frightened dog. A shot rang out and Phillip's yellow eyes re-focussed on the Sheriff, as he rapidly chambering another round into his hunting rifle. The beast darted back into the cell-block just as Beazel got off another round, the bullet splintering the wood of the door. The sound of breaking glass followed a few seconds later and Beazel swore under his breath, racing out to his car.

* * * * *

Deep within William Peeg's mansion, the playful sounds of Prokofiev echoed round the elaborate ballroom. Peeg sat at his concert piano, his trotter-like hands nimbly dancing over the keys with a dexterity that belied their turgid appearance. Having allowed Maxwell to retire early, William had elected to fill the remainder of his evening with sonatas, carefully contemplating the day's unexpected events in the key of A-minor.

At the sound of breaking glass, he halted mid-bar and turned to stare at the unkempt black shape which now stepped in through his window. Covered in coarse dark hair and about the size of a man, the creature alternated between walking upright and scurrying forward on all fours, its sharp claws clacking disharmoniously across the mahogany floor.

William rose slowly, not wishing to alarm the beast, and backed up against his piano, breath coming in staccato gasps. As the beast drew near, his hand unwittingly came down upon a collection of keys and the piano let out a fearful plink, its off-key shriek mirroring that of its owner as the wolf-like creature bounded forward. William's death scream came out as one long unending note of pure terror, rattling the remaining windows as he squealed out his last. Blood spattered across the polished keys of the piano, red on black/white, and then came the quiet, the only sound the slow pant of the beast as it padded back out into the darkness.

\* \* \* \* \*

No more than a hundred yards away, Jiggs moshed his head to a very different kind of music. His flattened snout rose and fell to the angry thrash of Metallica, music growling from the speakers of his straw hut studio as he pounded the desktop with drum sticks in time to the beat. Just as the music reached another delirious crescendo, the wall of the studio exploded in a cyclone of loose straw and fur and something large and black careened into the drum kit. Snared for a moment, the creature thrashed about amongst cymbals and pedals before righting itself and stalking hungrily forward. Jiggs' scream was lost amidst an angry guitar solo as he sank to his knees, feeling the beast's hot breath cloud his face.

"Why?" he managed to sob.

'I hunt, therefore I am' sang the reply from the speakers, and then the feasting began.

\* \* \* \* \*

Beazel's cruiser screeched to a halt outside the Peeg Estate moments later. Clambering out of the car, the frantic Sheriff ignored the chorus of Ozzy's Bark at the Moon coming through the trees, and darted inside the already unlocked main gate. Beyond lay an expansive garden, surrounded by narrow cloisters which offered several choice spots in which to conceal himself. No sooner had he positioned himself by a nearby stone pillar, did Phillip's hulking form skulk across the open gateway and sniff cautiously at the night air. The still flashing lights of the squad car illuminated the beast's shaggy outline in alternating blue and red, switching Phillip between hero and villain.

With a low clunk, the main door of the house swung open and the corpulent form of Elmer Peeg emerged from within, his portly frame clad in a fine burgundy smoking jacket. Upon seeing the beast in the gateway, he produced a solitary match and lit the cigar he held snug in one hand. As Phillip lunged forward, intent on fulfilling his bloodlust, a single shot rang out, the bullet catching him square in the side and bringing him down.

Elmer snorted in amusement as Beazel stepped warily out from the shadows and approached the creature with rifle still trained. The Sheriff watched in amazement as Phillip transformed back to a man, the coarse hide of hair shed to reveal that blood-spattered flesh lay beneath.

"I'm sorry," Beazel whispered, kneeling beside him. "I didn't have a choice."

Phillip's eyes opened weakly, no longer yellow but blue.

"There's always a choice," he whispered.

As Elmer Peeg's grotesque shadow fell over them both, Beazel solemnly watched Phillip die and realized for the first time what true courage was.

Peeg squealed with delight and bit off the end of his cigar, turning to plod victoriously back into his fortress.

Standing, Beazel chambered one final round and took careful aim, lining up the Devil in his trembling sights.

"It's my choice," he acknowledged, before pulling the trigger.

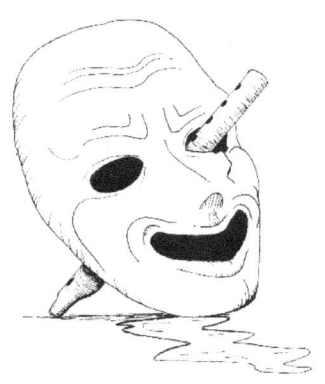

FIDDLER'S GREEN

by E. M. Eastick

Stephen Sly posed side-on in front of the hallway mirror and unbuttoned his suit jacket with a practiced flourish. He nodded to imaginary fans, smiled to imaginary paparazzi, and ran a hand up the imaginary backside of a sparkly, big-haired starlet with chest enhancements.

The jangle of keys interrupted his daydream. "You're going to be late." His wife, Helen, leaned against the kitchen bench and dangled a key ring shaped like a miniature Oscar award in front of her nose.

Stephen joined his wife in the kitchen. "I'll get the part of Philippe, anyway. My agent's chummy with the producer."

"Is that right?" Helen raised her eyebrows. "I heard Finlay Goode was auditioning, too."

"What?" Stephen went cold. "Why does he want a role in a low-budget film like *Fiddler's Green*? Why is he even in town? Last I heard, he was making it big performing live in Vegas."

"His mother's sick. Finlay came back to look after her." Helen studied her fingernails. "I guess a role in a local production would be perfect for him right now."

Stephen quickly buttoned his jacket. "And what about me? I *need* this role." He'd heard a number of big shot Hollywood agents were hovering round the town. "*We* need this role. There's bills to pay..."

Helen laughed. "My salary pays the bills just fine."

"But you're only a teacher."

Helen sighed as she opened the fridge and pulled out a pint of milk.

"How do you know about Finlay anyway?"

Helen settled at the breakfast table and poured milk into a steaming cup of coffee. "Carol and I sat next to each other at the hairdressers yesterday. We had a good old chat."

Carol. Stephen imagined the leading lady's mane of golden hair being tussled and teased by lucky hairdresser hands.

"Earth to Stephen—" The keys jingled again.

Stephen blinked Carol out of his mind and accepted the keys his wife held over her shoulder. "Wish me luck." He pecked her on the cheek and shot through the door.

Instead of climbing into his Honda, Stephen marched down the driveway and turned with a skip onto the sidewalk. Three blocks later, he slowed as he neared the brick bungalow Carol shared with a friend. When the front door swung open, Stephen puffed out his chest and lifted a hand in greeting.

"Hi, Stephen." A girl with lank brown hair pulled back in a messy pony tail waved nervously as she trotted down the porch steps and hurried to the road. Stephen vaguely recalled she attended high school with him and now worked at the library. Her name escaped him.

"Oh, hi ... there," said Stephen dropping his hand. "Is Carol about?"

"Just left." Abruptly, the girl stopped beside him. "She told me you and Finlay Goode are trying out for the lead role this morning." She offered a freckly smile before scurrying down the sidewalk. "Good luck with *that*."

Didn't anyone in this town appreciate his talent? Stephen felt his jaw tighten as he watched the librarian disappear behind Frankie's Barber Shop, the old-fashioned candy pole twirling like an illusion in her wake.

He turned east on Fifth and followed the railway tracks until he reached the trail that led to the Talky River footbridge. If he cut across the empty lot behind Chuck's Hardware, he could intercept Carol before she reached the theatre. Maybe there was still time to convince her that he and she would make the perfect leading couple.

The narrow river that divided the town rumbled softly as Stephen neared the footbridge. A tall man with fine, blond hair leaned against the rail, blocking the way, and seemed to study the rush of water below with some intensity.

He straightened when Stephen approached. "Good morning, Stephen," said Finlay Goode with the gusto typical of a stage performer. "On your way to the audition?"

Stephen groaned. His stomach cramped.

Finlay combed his hair with elegant fingers and adjusted his tie. "I hear Carol's to play Isabella Du Bois. She's perfect for the role, don't you think?" When Stephen tried to step past him, Finlay raised both hands and bid him to stop. "Is everything all right, Stephen? You look pale."

Pale!? He'd spent hours and hundreds of dollars at Lou's tanning salon over the last few weeks.

"In fact, you look positively ill, old boy. I'm sure we could postpone auditions if you need to rest."

"*We*?" stammered Stephen.

"Well, yes. I know Harry, the producer, quite well."

"Sounds like you have an unfair advantage." Stephen struggled to control the shaky snarl in his voice.

"Harry is a fair and reasonable man; he'll understand." Finlay placed a hand on Stephen's shoulder. "I really think you should lie down. You look terrible."

Stephen swiped the hand from his shoulder. "Oh, you'd like that, wouldn't you? To have me out of the way so you can have Carol all to yourself."

"What!? No. Come on, Stephen, calm down, will you."

"I'll calm down all right. Just as soon as I deal with you." Stephen grabbed Finlay by the shoulder, jerked him to the bridge's rail, and flung him over the side. The scream stopped suddenly when Finlay's body hit the rocks by the water's edge and came to rest half in and half out of the river.

Stephen wiped the sweat from his forehead as he stared at the figure beneath the bridge. A sharply broken bone, displaced when Finlay's hip crashed into a knobby outcrop, jutted up from the mauled flesh. A swirl of current licked at Finlay's fractured skull and tugged his left arm, as if easing the body into a watery coffin. Stephen winced at the mess in the otherwise picturesque surroundings and hoped the river would hurry up and claim the body.  As he hustled to the audition, he refused to think of the sick old woman who awaited her son's return.

* * * * *

Six months later, the crew of *Fiddler's Green* scattered to enjoy a thirty minute break before the next shoot.  Stephen allowed Carol to hug his arm as they walked down Main Street on their way to Sunshine Café.  Matt and Dave, Stephen's old class mates, stepped from Chuck's Hardware and nodded cordially.  Stephen squared his shoulders and nodded back—how the old boys wished they were in his position.

Stephen ushered Carol into the café, where they chose a table by the window and ordered lattes.  "You were great this morning," he said, searching her eyes for mutual adoration.

"How's Helen coping with your working these long hours?"

Stephen blinked.  "Who?"

"Helen.  Your wife.  Remember her?"

Carol had cleaned her face of make-up, ready for it to be reapplied for the next scene, and looked more radiant than ever.  "Oh, her," said Stephen.  "Actually, we've split up."

"Really?"

"She doesn't understand the actor's life."

"But you were an actor when she married you, weren't you?"

Fluttering the question away with his hand, he said, "I'm ready for a new direction in life.  I've felt this way ever since the audition for *Fiddler's Green*."

Carol smiled like the sun. "I'm really enjoying playing opposite you. You make such a great Philippe." And then her face darkened. "Though I often wonder what happened to Finlay Goode. He was such a handsome man. And so talented."

"And he left his poor sick mother all alone like that," Stephen reminded her.

Carol dropped her chin and peered out from under lowered eyelids. "I heard you went to see her."

Stephen looked out the window and hoped the heat in his face wasn't noticeable. "Who told you?"

"It's a small town," said Carol shrugging. "My housemate's in a book club with the nurse Finlay arranged for his mother."

When Stephen remained silent, his attention held by a golden retriever trotting past the window, Carol leaned over the table. "You really were concerned about the old lady, weren't you?"

Stephen cleared his throat and shifted in his seat. "After Finlay's— disappearance, I just wanted to make sure she was being looked after. I couldn't help thinking of my own mother in that situation."

Soft fingertips stroked his hand. "That's so sweet." Carol's beautiful face was torn between admiration and anguish. "Poor Mrs. Goode, dying without ever knowing what happened to her son."

Stephen sat up. "She died?"

"Oh yes, last month. Didn't you know? Finlay wasn't at the funeral, so one can only assume something terrible has happened to him." She sighed. "So sad..."

The two sat quietly and sipped their coffees. When the air between them seemed too thick to breathe, Stephen felt the moment was right. "Carol, would you like to—"

"Say, Stephen, did you hear about the changes Harry wants to make to *Fiddler's Green*?" The sparkle returned to her eyes.

"Changes? But it's almost done, isn't it?"

"Apparently there's been a budget increase, so they want to make it into a musical."

"What!?"

"I know. Isn't it exciting?" Carol bounced up and down like a jubilant school girl.

"It's absurd. We can't sing."

"Of course we can." She flashed perfect teeth in a smile. "The actors of today need to be multi-skilled. You can sing, can't you?"

Stephen couldn't bear to admit to being tone deaf. "Of course I can."

"Of course you can," repeated Carol. "Philippe's a musician, for goodness' sake. It makes perfect sense to make *Fiddler's Green* into a musical." She glanced at the gold-chain watch draped over her wrist and stood. "Time to get back to work. Oh, I can't wait to meet the musical director." She skipped to the door and stepped into the street. Stephen followed with none of her enthusiasm. He didn't bother leaving a tip.

* * * * *

The musical director's name was Lenny Justice. Stroking his pointy beard, he flounced onto the set, a meticulous reproduction of a nineteenth century French boudoir, and spouted directions. "The score is wonderful, darlings," he said as he kissed each cast and crew member in turn. "Now here's what we're going to do."

38

Stephen edged to the back of the production team. When Carol saw, or rather heard, how badly he sung, surely she would lose interest in him. He had spent the last three nights without sleep and had bitten his fingernails ragged in dread of this moment.

Lenny continued to talk. He spent an hour fussing over Carol, introducing her to the new musical component of her role and sampling her voice. Carol beamed when Lenny raved about her singing talents.

"Now where is the leading man?" said Lenny scanning the crew. Stephen ducked behind the frizzy black hair of a camera operator of indeterminate sex. "Ah, there you are. Come, come." Lenny latched onto Stephen's arm and dragged him to center stage.

Stephen swallowed. Should he admit he couldn't sing, or try to bluff his way through? He waited to hear what Lenny had to say.

"Philippe is a musician," began Lenny. His hands rolled in front of his chest as if to build the character as he talked. "He is a man of passion and impulse."

Stephen hoped that Carol had stepped out to the ladies' room, but when he glanced at the faces crowded round him, there she was, bright and beautiful, staring back at him with trusting blue eyes. He tried to capture her perfection in a mental snapshot before the disappointment struck.

"But he is a man of few words," continued Lenny. "Strong and silent."

"That's right!" cheered Stephen with a surge of hope.

"And so," announced Lenny, "Philippe will not sing."

"Wahoo!" Stephen clamped his hand over his mouth. "I mean..." he mumbled through his fingers. "That's a shame."

Lenny frowned and then smiled. "Instead, you will play a whistle."

Stephen let the words sink in. A whistle? That wasn't so bad. He learned the clarinet in middle school, only because Miss Garibaldi was the music teacher, but he learned it, nevertheless. "I can do that," he said triumphantly. Carol clapped her hands and bounced her excited bounce, her golden hair leaping about.

"Good, good," said Lenny. "Philippe is a very special character, and so I have a very special whistle for him to play. It is to be his whistle; his signature piece."

"Okay," said Stephen slowly.

"Voila." From inside his coat, Lenny whipped out a long, pale tube shaped and molded at the top and slightly curled at the bottom. Six neatly drilled finger holes dotted the length.

Stephen accepted the piece and examined it. "This looks a lot like—bone."

"It is, Stephen. Isn't it magnificent?"

"It's a little creepy, if you ask me, which you did, by the way."

Lenny laughed. "Some cultures believe that bones can sing."

"What cultures?"

Lenny paused. "Never mind," he said quickly as he snatched the whistle from Stephen's hand. "If you really object, then we can forget the whistle. Perhaps Philippe should sing after all."

Stephen snatched the whistle back. "No, no, we needn't go that far. By creepy, I meant it's really interesting. You know?"

Lenny frowned again and stroked his little beard. "You have only one simple jingle to play," he said in a dubious tone. "You repeat it in several scenes."

"Like a signature piece."

"Quite," said Lenny, unimpressed by Stephen's brilliant deduction. "Do you think you can manage just one simple tune?"

Stephen chuffed a single chuff. "We modern actors are multi-skilled, don't you know? Of course I can play one simple tune." He examined the whistle more closely, and then raised it to his face and sniffed it. "Is it, you know, treated?"

"Treated?"

"Like, safe?"

"Safe?"

"It smells a little funny. You didn't just find it somewhere, did you? It is a proper musical instrument, isn't it?"

"Of course it is," said Lenny indignantly. "Hand-crafted locally by the artisan who runs the craft stall near Talky Bridge."

"That old hag?" When Stephen noticed the disapproving looks on the faces of the onlookers, particularly Carol, he cleared his throat. "I mean, isn't that nice old lady clever." He gave the whistle another sniff.

"So, are you going to try it or not?" Lenny's delicate arms folded across his chest.

Carol was nodding sharp little nods. The sunny smile had returned to her face. Taking a deep breath, Stephen positioned his fingers over the holes and stuck the mouthpiece, shaped and molded with a clear resin, between his lips, and then blew.

The set fell silent. The bone whistle began to sing.

Stephen looked at Carol as he played. Her eyes glimmered with joyful tears. Her hands rested over her heart. Perfect, thought Stephen. Just perfect. With a tiny smile, he pulled the whistle from between his lips.

But the whistle kept on singing, and then words seemed to form in the sound, clear and delicate, like raindrops on tin: *. . . nights grow colder by the hour . . .*

"What's going on?" said Stephen staring at the bone as if it were a ticking bomb.

"It's singing," said Lenny, his eyes wide.

*. . . when envy burns and dreams go sour . . .*

"By itself?"

*. . . once a precious goodly flower . . .*

"Oh, it's beautiful," said Carol, who now stood beside them.

*. . . savaged by a darkly power . . .*

All ears honed in on the bone whistle in Stephen's hand. "It's just garble," he said.

"Shh," snapped Carol. "Listen."

The bone whistle sang louder: *Dreams will eat into your sleep; lust into your heart will creep; arrogance will bury deep; but murder takes your soul to keep.*

Stephen dropped the whistle, and it clattered on the floorboards, but it kept on singing. He felt the blood drain from his face. "This is ridic—"

"Shh," said Lenny and Carol together. The two bent forward to listen to the bone on the floor.

*Two men o'er the Talky stood, one for envy, one for Goode; river secrets understood; damned is Sly for killing Goode.*

The whistle fell silent. All eyes turned to Stephen.

"What does it mean?" said Carol quietly. "Stephen—?"

Stephen stared back into the accusing blue eyes and tried to swallow down the guilt, but his mouth was dry. "I never..." His eyes dropped to the whistle on the floor. "I never knew bones could sing."

Lenny shook his head as he pulled a phone from his pocket.

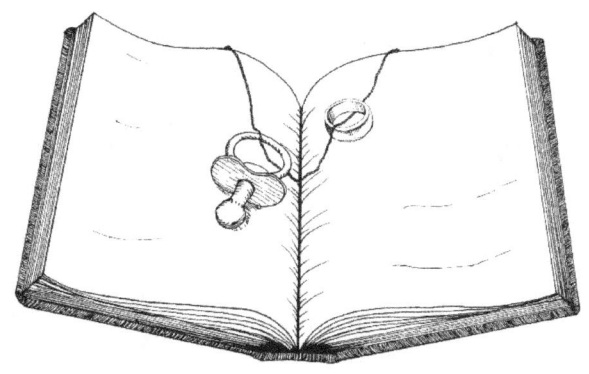

SNAPS

by Charie D. La Marr

Snaps. Hundreds of them every day. Snaps on diaper covers, onesies, sleepers, rompers. On and off all day long to change wet, smelly diapers. One day, I tried to count exactly how many snaps I opened and closed in a single day and gave up at seventy-five. That's more than 525 a week. Over 27,000 a year. Yes, other than being the mother of Trevor Ryan Patterson, Jr., I had no life.

A year earlier, I did. I was an account executive at a large Madison Avenue ad firm. You watch my commercials and read my print ads every day. I had breakfast meetings, lunch meetings, dinner meetings and meetings in between breakfast and lunch meetings. I spent hours with clients agonizing over the difference between Pantone 2602 and Pantone 2612 from the box of color swatches on the corner of my desk. By the way, Pantone 2602 and 2612 are both purple to you mere mortals. Blue-violet to those with degrees in art.

I agonized over slogans and product placement. I regularly suited up in my best Oscar de la Renta to drag boards into the President's conference room and try to sell—sell—sell to company executives who barely spoke English and spent more time staring at my boobs than looking at my ideas. I learned to bow and say things like, "Domo arrigato" and "Do xia" to out of town clients. Yes, I was on the fast track—working my way up the ladder of success toward that corner office and those letters AVP on my door.

And then I got pregnant and everything changed. The father, a Wall Street broker and really nice guy, decided to do the honorable thing and marry me. And so I dragged my ever-growing stomach into the office every day until I couldn't wear heels anymore and then switched to flats and worked another month. Then I went on maternity leave—another word for Dante's third level of Hell. Oh, don't get me wrong, I love the little guy. He's cute as a button and melts my heart every time he smiles. It was the boredom I couldn't take.

I tried it all. Reading, Sudoku, crosswords, game shows, soap operas, yoga exercise videos. Nothing seemed to kill that monotony I felt away from my office. I even tried sitting in the park with the little one, but I swear if I heard one more mommy talking about how many ounces their little darling drank, how many hours they slept or how they made their own baby food, I was ready to shove their hands in a blender and puree them. Nothing's worse than mommy talk.

Trevor, Sr. tried to be supportive. He offered to babysit a few nights a week so I could go out with the girls from work. But it was hard to get up the energy after a long day in the baby trenches and even harder to fit into anything remotely decent from my closet.  The one time I did try, I came home to find the phone ringing, the TV blasting, the baby screaming, the dog in the refrigerator and Daddy happily napping with one hand stuffed down his pants.  Live and learn.

My next choice was the Internet.  Despite having owned and worked on computers since almost the very beginning, I was still what they called a "noob" when it came to things like Facebook, Twitter, YouTube, and the rest.  I was totally unaware there was a whole world out there literally living their lives on the Internet.  With the help of a kid in the building, I learned about a few chat rooms and made some connections with other bored mommies, but when it got to the point that I was literally getting messages like, "I went to the bathroom without the baby today! Tomorrow, I'm going to try for #2!"  I was just too disgusted to continue.  So one day, I disconnected my account, along with the four thousand pictures of adorable puppies and kittens I'd saved up.  That was tough, believe me.  I still miss those cute little guys.

My next option was surfing the 'Net.  Back to the kid in the building for more lessons.  In no time at all, I was buying adorable baby things and cheap jewelry on eBay.  I visited sites of former clients to see how crappy their websites looked.  I sent Trevor cute little messages at work.  I Googled old boyfriends until I started to feel like a stalker.  When that got boring, I started just surfing.  One day, I just seemed to go crazy, going from one site to another, following ads and recommended sites to see where it led me.

That's when I found it.  "WRITE THE NEXT GREAT AMERICAN NOVEL!  Only $19.99!!  Self-publish it for all your friends and family.  A great Christmas gift!!!  They'll all be wondering where your newfound talent came from!"

46

I clicked on the site—a rather low-end job with simple instructions. All I had to do was pay the money and start answering the prompts. When I was done, the site would print out my masterpiece. They even recommended two or three vanity presses to send my book to. It sounded like fun.

So, I got out my handy-dandy Amex Card and ordered. For a user name, I chose "BoredMommy." I chose a password and clicked "Yes, I have read the instructions in their entirety." I really hadn't. Nobody ever does. Then I went to work. The first prompt came up. "Type of story," it asked. I used the pull-down menu and selected "Historical Romance." That sounded like what I could expect for my twenty bucks. "Name your protagonist," it asked me next. I thought for a moment and then typed, "Theodore Wellington." It asked for a woman's name. I typed, "Miranda Everett," the prettiest girl in my eighth grade Science class. "Name your antagonist," it asked. I thought about using the name of the guy who knocked me up and got me into this whole mess, but instead, I selected, "Edward Forrester"—my first boss. What a jackass he was.

The questions continued. I chose London for locale and 1840 for my time frame. They kept coming. Miranda had two sisters—both younger. Edward was a wealthy land baron. Theodore was a schoolteacher whose parents were both deceased. Edward lived on an estate called "Forrester Grove" and Miranda lived at "Everettfaire". I continued.

The next thing I knew, I came to the final question, "Name your book" and answered just as the baby started crying. I'd been answering through his entire nap—nearly five hundred questions, each one of them a decision about the "book" I was writing.

## It's a Grimm Life

I got up, changed and fed him and put him in his little swing to play for a while so I could start to think about what to defrost for dinner. I glanced at the computer. "Print Now!" was flashing over and over. I filled the printer tray up and went off to the kitchen. Five times, I had to go back and refill it, but when it finally stopped, there were nearly four hundred pages sitting in the paper tray and the printer was wheezing. I left it there. I'd save it for the following day's naptime to read.

The following day, Master Trevor decided to reward me for the lovely warm lunch bottle I fed him by giving it back to me—all over my clothes and hair—while he screamed bloody murder. What are you supposed to do in a situation like that? From the mess on the two of us and the floor, I assumed he threw up the entire eight ounces. Do you give them another one? Or do you just hold off until the next feeding? Why don't babies come with instruction books? They come with books on what to name them, but not books that answered the really key issues.

I bathed him and put him in clean clothes and he fell asleep, so that answered the re-feeding question. There was no way I was waking him up to feed him again. Instead I tiptoed into the bedroom and stripped naked, stuffing my sour smelling clothes into the hamper. Then I ran like hell to the shower. By the time my hair was clean and dry, the little man was awake and screaming again. I decided the next time I was in the drug store I'd buy a few bathing caps for feedings. Nothing's worse than the smell of spoiled formula in your hair. Trust me, you could go to the cemetery and dig up somebody who's been dead for twenty years and it would smell better.

A couple days later, I finally got around to reading *The Bride Wore Black*, my Great American Novel. It wasn't half bad. In fact, it was kind of entertaining. As a joke, I sent it to my college roommate, Jackie. She has three kids and belongs to about five romance novel reading groups. I sent it along with a note that said, "This is a hoot—read it!"

She wrote me back about a week later. "I laughed, I cried, I peed my pants. I busted a corset. Seriously, you wrote that Angela? That's freaking amazing. It shouldn't surprise me though. You wrote some good stuff in college. Send it to Maggie Jackson, remember her? She's a big New York literary agent now. Let her have a look. I think you have something there."

I looked Mags up on the Internet and called. We had a few laughs remembering some of our wild college days and she told me to send it. She couldn't promise me anything but her honest opinion.

I was totally shocked when two weeks later, I got a contract in the mail. I had a big time New York literary agent. I signed and returned it immediately. Maggie called the following day to say she knew I'd sign and had already shown the first chapter around to a couple publishers and there was interest. As it ended up, there was a bidding war and when the dust settled, *The Bride Wore Black* had a home at a major publisher and I had a big fat advance check.

The next nine months were a virtual whirlwind. Except for a few lunches with Maggie, most of the work on the book was done via Internet and FedEx. Before I knew it, I was approving a galley, looking at a copy of the cover and discussing a book signing in New York to launch it. And all because I was going crazy at home alone with the baby, counting snaps on sleepers.

\* \* \* \* \*

## It's a Grimm Life

The book launch was held at a New York City branch of a large bookstore chain. It was promoted a lot in the papers and even in some romance novel magazines. It was a big deal, with sparkling cider and hors d'oeuvres, and me all in black wearing a fancy fascinator hat with a little veil. I starved myself for three months to get into that dress. Trevor, Sr. was in the front row beaming, sitting next to Jackie, who flew in for the occasion and Maggie, who was getting 15% of everything I made. At the last minute, the babysitter backed out on us, so little Trevor—now known as Little Terror—was in the green room with a bookstore employee watching him. He was walking and into everything, so we had a portable playpen.

I didn't know there were that many romance novel fans in New York. I figured city girls were more reality based. But apparently a lot of girls in New York went to bed at night with a romance novel, a pint of Godiva ice cream and a vibrator. Come to think of it, I probably did that myself a couple of times. Only with best-sellers. I signed until I thought my hand would fall off. I smiled and greeted everyone and talked to the girls from my former office. Everything was going great until I looked up and saw this strange little man standing in front of me holding a book.

Not even five feet tall, he was dressed in a royal purple suit with a lilac shirt and a gold bow tie. A large red carnation was poked through the buttonhole of his lapel. His hair was the color of straw and looked like it— dry and jutting out in every direction like it had never seen a comb or hairbrush. He was a candidate for some of those fancy haircare products I used to do ads for. His nose was long with an upturn at the end, his cheeks were rouged and he wore a bit of lipstick. And he was wearing glasses with purple lenses that would have made Elton John crawl through burning coals to own. But as odd as he looked, nobody in the room seemed to be paying any attention to him.

"Good evening," he said, holding out his hand to me. "I'm the author."

"Oh," I replied. "I didn't know there was another book signing going on tonight. What's the name of your book?"

He held up a copy of *The Bride Wore Black*. "This one," he said.

I laughed. "That's funny. Actually I'm the author of that book. My first novel. Would you like me to sign it for you?"

"No, thank you. And I am the author. Perhaps you remember my website, 'Write the Next Great American Novel for $19.99?' You paid with an American Express Card. I have the number right here if you like," he said, reaching into his jacket pocket. "You also checked the box saying you read all the instructions. But obviously you hadn't. They clearly stated that the site was for entertainment purposes only and that the books the site produced could only be published by vanity presses as gifts for family and friends. Publishing professionally was strictly forbidden. Did you read all that?"

"Actually, that was quite a while ago, and I don't entirely remember." I looked at the long line waiting for signed books. "Look, why don't you sit over there and wait until I'm done? Then we can discuss this some more. If necessary, I can bring my agent and my lawyer into the conversation. Both of them are here tonight."

"I'll be quite happy to wait. Only I don't think it will be entirely necessary to bring in your big guns. This is a personal matter between the two of us. I am sure that together we can arrive at a simple resolution. Please, take your time, dear lady. Greet your esteemed guests. I have nowhere to go. I'll be here when you're done."

A little while later when all the signing was done and the schmoozing had begun, I told my husband and friends to wait while I talked to someone privately. I motioned to the little man and led him into the green room. Someone was sitting there reading while my son was sleeping. I told her that she could go. We sat down on the couch.

"Can I get you something to drink?" I asked.

"Do you have sassafras tea? If not, lapsang souchong will do. With organic honey from free ranging bees if you have it."

"Sorry," I said. "We have water, sparkling water and sparkling cider. Any of those hit your fancy?"

"Actually, no," he said. "I'd rather get down to business."

He took a folded page from his inside jacket pocket. Actually it was three folded pages. "Let's see now. It begins with the party of the first part hereafter known as THE PURCHASER agrees to pay $19.99 to the party of the second part hereafter known as THE OWNER ..." He flipped over to the next page. "Now, this is the statement and instructions that are at the bottom of my website. The ones to which you checked, [Yes]. The PURCHASER hereby agrees that he/she has read all of the above and agrees to abide by the rules of THE OWNER by checking [Yes] before proceeding. I know you checked [Yes] because the programming is set so you must check [Yes] in order to access the site. Therefore, undoubtedly and without question, you checked [Yes]."

"Okay, so I checked [Yes], people always check [Yes] when they see those things, don't they? It's kind of automatic. You never get into a site without checking [Yes]. Yours is not unique."

"Yes, but did you read what you checked [Yes] to? If I would venture a guess, I'd say you didn't read it in its entirely, did you?"

"Yes, I mean no, I mean maybe I didn't read it in its entirety. I paid the money and I was very interested to see what your site was. Don't you think most people check [Yes] and go directly to the first page?"

"No, I mean yes. Actually, I mean no, I don't believe they check [Yes] unless they mean it. I assume most people read what it says and abide by that which they have checked [Yes] to. Especially since you're the first one who's crossed the line and failed to obey the rules. Therefore, I have to refer to page three of the statement where the penalty clause is stated in full. You were also required to initial there, which you did. It clearly states that should you fail to abide by the rules, I, Momus T. Romersklinstill, am entitled to compensation."

"Well," I said, reaching for the page. "I'll be happy to discuss this with my agent and lawyer in the morning. I'm sure we can arrive at some sort of a settlement. However, I must point out to you that I did pay the twenty bucks for access to your site, and the fact is you didn't write the book. You merely wrote the computer program that allowed me to write the book."

"You didn't write it either," he said. "You merely answered a series of questions that allowed the program to devise the book. And, I might point out again, you answered the first question incorrectly."

"Well, we'll just see about that when my lawyer sues you," I said, my bravado on the rise. "You have no proof it was me anyway. The credit card I used had my maiden name on it and I registered with a fake name. Besides, the editor made a lot of changes to the book. There are characters that aren't even in it anymore. The locale was changed and so was the time period. You've got nothing."

"Sues me?" He laughed sardonically. "You'd really do that? Sue me in open court and admit to the world and your publisher that you're a complete fraud and not the author of *The Bride Wore Black*? You'll be the laughingstock of the publishing world! I think it best if we just proceed directly to the penalty clause and leave everyone else out of this."

"Suppose I did?" I asked. "Exactly what does the penalty clause say? I'm not saying I didn't read it; it was just quite a while ago. Maybe I just forgot what it said. So why don't you refresh my memory?"

He sat back and crossed his legs. He was actually wearing leopard skin platform shoes that added about three or four inches to his height. I wondered what boys' department actually sold clothes like that. Not one I'd be visiting any time soon. "I'd think you'd remember something like that, Mrs. Patterson. It simply states that I, Momus T. Romersklinstill, am entitled to take possession of your firstborn child, naturally. Isn't that how it usually works in fairy tales with you vain, silly women who attempt to do things you aren't capable of?"

"Actually, that's the third time, you Rumplestiltskin wanna-be. You don't scare me. If you're following the script, the first two times are a necklace and a ring," I said.

"Yeah, well I'm not really in need of any cheap baubles at the moment. So let's just cut to the chase, shall we? And now, Master Patterson and I will be leaving."

He got up. I got up. I grabbed a sparkling cider bottle. "Make one move toward that baby and you're going to meet your maker, whoever that might be, you little twerp."

"Actually, you are wrong about that, too. Twerps are something completely different in the fairy world."

I held the bottle over my head. It was almost full. I stood there shaking while carbonated apple juice ran down my face and soaked my new dress. I looked like a damn fool, but that ridiculous little manikin was not touching that baby. "What are you, one of those pedo-bears? Do you know what the penalty is in New York these days for child kidnapping?

Ready to become a registered sex offender? Touch that kid and I'll scream so loud the sprinkler system will go off!"

He stood there a moment in silence. It was clear I'd won that round.

"Very well, Mrs. Patterson, but I must warn you. Do not attempt to use my site again or I'll follow through on the penalty clause. Master Trevor would make a wonderful companion for a lonely little man like me. He'll be quite comfortable living under my bridge."

"Ha! So you are a troll!"

"Yes, ma'am. A troll who knows how to write code quite well. However, I find it quite lonely."

I wanted to suggest eHarmony, but it didn't seem like a good time. All I really wanted to do was get home and wash my hair before I turned into a candy apple.

"I'll be blocking you from my site anyway, Mrs. Patterson. This is where you and I part ways. For now. I won't be used by a fraud like you for your own ill-gotten gain. But I have a feeling that despite blocking you, one day we'll meet again. Good evening."

He walked out the door and closed it quietly behind him. I ran to the playpen to check on Trevor. He was sleeping peacefully. The little guy slept all the way through his attempted kidnapping. What a trooper.

My husband walked in, seeing me leaning over the playpen dripping cider all over the place.

"My God, Angela, what happened to you? Usually someone else pours the champagne on your head. You don't do it to yourself."

"Didn't you see that man who just left? Scaled down version of Prince? Purple suit? Leopard shoes? Elton John glasses?"

"No, Angela. I was standing outside the door talking to your agent. I figured you were packing up the baby to leave. I was waiting for you to ask me to come in and lug the playpen to the car. Nobody left this room. I was right outside the door the whole time."

I felt like a complete fool. Had I made it all up? Maybe the whole thing was just too much stress on me. There really was no Momus T. Romersklinstill, nasty little troll and cheap software designer. I went home and slept easy that night. Although I made sure the alarm was turned on and the baby monitor was up as loud as it went.

Several months later, Trevor and I were napping when the phone rang.

"Hullo?" I said, still half asleep.

"Did I catch you sleeping?" It was my 15% richer agent, Maggie. "I was just wondering, what are we working on these days?"

"Gee, I don't know, Maggie. Is this a trick question? What are you working on these days?"

"No, silly, I meant you. I talked to someone at your publisher the other day and they're wondering how your new book is coming along."

"What new book is that, Maggie?"

"Umm ... the second book in your three book contract? Or did you forget about that? Angela, please tell me you're writing something."

"Oh, I am. It's not really pulled together yet. But it will be soon. It's getting there. No title yet. But it's going to be good, I promise. I'll get back to you in about two weeks with a first draft. How does that work for you?"

"Terrific," Maggie said. "Because they're on my case about this. And remember you're only as good as your next book."

"Isn't it you're only as good as your last book?"

"Whatever," Maggie said a bit petulantly. "Just get back to me, okay?"

I hung up and grabbed my purse, running to the computer. I needed to get back on that site. There was no way I could write a book. If it was more than a ten-word slogan for a product, I was completely lost. I logged in and searched my history until I found it. Praying it was still there; I pushed the button and waited.

"ACCESS DENIED"

How could the little troll do that? I didn't even use my name or anything. I couldn't be denied. I needed to get on that site and punch out another book—like yesterday. I was in serious trouble. *The Bride Wore Black* was a crossover best seller. It surpassed the romance novel market and moved into contemporary fiction. I had a lot of glowing reviews and even made some bestseller lists. There was talk of a mini-series. How was I going to explain the best thing I ever wrote was, "Fairhair Shampoo—It Brings Out The Princess In You?"

Then I remembered Eddie. Eddie lived one floor above us. He was fourteen years old and knew more about computers than Bill Gates and Steve Jobs combined. He taught me all I knew about the Internet. When Trevor got hit with a virus (from surfing porn), Eddie was able to retrieve 99% of his data and keep his boss from finding out about his little 'accident'. And he did it in about three hours.

I threw on some clothes, grabbed the baby and went upstairs to get Eddie. He came down and tried the site, getting the same message. He tried a few times. Same thing. I started to hyperventilate.

"Well, Mrs. P, there are a couple things we can do. We can try resetting your modem. Most of the time, that'll let you back in. But there's a chance he'd be able to trace it back to you again."

"No!" I said. "He cannot know I was on his site!"

"You could get another provider, but that would take a while. Or we could wardrive."

"Wardrive? That sounds like serious hacking. I don't want to get in any trouble. And I don't want you in trouble." I pictured the Feds busting the door down. Over a romance novel?

"Hell no, Mrs. P! It just means someone nearby doesn't have their computer protected. We can look for an open Wi-Fi network and click it. Then we'd be kind of borrowing their service for a while. Trust me— plenty of people in this building are too dumb to use passwords. I do it all the time. No big deal. When my parents cancelled our service because I failed English, I was back on in an hour."

"Incredible," I said. "But there's still the chance it could be traced back to my building. Even if it is a small chance. I don't know how smart this guy is. But he's pretty strange, trust me."

"Then your best bet is a cyber café. You go to any convenience store and buy a pre-paid credit card. Sit at a café and do whatever it is you need to do. You can make a CD there and bring it home to print if you want to save a little money."

"That's perfect, Eddie! You saved my life! And by the way, do you wardrive us?"

He shrugged. "I used to. But when I fixed Mr. Patterson's computer after that virus, I gave you passwords."

"Oh yeah, MRSP204."

"That's okay. Over half the building is without passwords. I manage. Then there's the building next door. I hit a lot of them up, too."

The next day, I got a babysitter and took off on my secret mission. I went to a café clear across town with a purse full of blank CD's and a brand new pre-paid credit card. I had a plan.

I brought a whole list of ridiculous names, crazy locations and other stupid details all prepared. Even a really dumb title. When I got home, I'd put in the names I had in mind, change the locale and details-- even change the time in history. With a new title, and some crafty editing, it would be unrecognizable as one of the little troll's $20 books. And while I was at it, I did a third book and stored it on a CD for future use.

I waited two weeks and shipped it off to my agent. She was overjoyed. *Rain in the Afternoon* was even better than *The Bride Wore Black*. A guaranteed best-seller. And sure enough, it debuted on the Times list. Not at the top, but high enough that Maggie bought a new car.

I convinced the publisher to start my book tour on the West Coast and work my way back home. Little Trevor went to stay with my parents. My mother's remarried, so the little freak couldn't even get to him through my maiden name. Everything was going great.

Then he showed up in Dallas. In an orange Western suit with fringed sleeves, hot pink cowboy boots and a yellow cowboy hat. Obviously, he was in his warm color period. Once again, he introduced himself to me as the author and once again, we found ourselves chatting in a private room at the bookstore.

"You're full of it, Momus, my man," I said, making sure the bottle on the table in front of me was empty. "I wrote this one. Check your records. You have nothing."

"My site was accessed at an Internet café on the Upper West Side. It produced a book called *Bill and Hillary Go to the Zoo*. The plot is surprisingly similar, although none of the names are the same, the locale is different and it takes place in the 1890s. I can't prove it, but I know this book came from my site."

"Sorry, Momus. I live on the lower East Side. That's not my neighborhood. I have a complete set of notes, outlines and drafts on my hard drive—date stamped. I wrote it. But I tell you what, here—take this ring as a token of my appreciation. The ring was the second thing the princess gave the little troll who spun straw into gold, right?"

"Don't mock me!" Momus screamed. "I'll tear that site down! You'll never use me to write another book! Do you hear me?"

"Be my guest," I said. "Do your worst. I wrote this book all by myself. You don't scare me, little troll. So take your ring and go back under the bridge where you came from. I think we're finished here."

He stormed out of the room. A minute or two later, Maggie walked in.

"Hey, did you see the Sunshine Cowboy?"

"Huh?" she asked.

"The little dude in the orange suit with the pink cowboy boots and yellow half-gallon hat? He just left."

"Angela, nobody just left. Are you losing it on me, girlfriend? Because we can cancel the rest of this tour and go home. Maybe you're missing the little guy too much. You're not going Sylvia Plath on me, are you?"

"Come on, you couldn't have missed him! They could see him all the way to Ft. Worth!"

"Nope, nobody out of the ordinary. Just a bunch of typical Dallas JR's and Sue Ellens with big hair."

I stared at the door. "Never mind. It was nothing," I said.

The third book was the most important of all. With that one, I wasn't playing for jewelry; I was playing for my firstborn child. I had to make absolutely sure it was well disguised. It would take time to do it right. As soon as I got back to New York, I opened up the file entitled, *The Prince and the Harlot* and got busy. I visited dozens of writing sites and learned how to do outlines and story arcs. I made character studies. I even registered for a couple Creative Writing classes at City College under a fictitious name.

And the more I learned, the better I got. I made shifts in the plot. I moved characters and scenes around. I changed the setting to Chicago in the '20s and spent a ton of time in the library and online researching. And the more I did, the farther away from Momus T. Romersklinstill's hokey little story I got and the more I started to write myself. When I was done, *City Harmony* bore absolutely no resemblance to the cheesy little $20 story. It had become my own. And I had the notes and backup material to prove it.

When I turned the first draft over to Maggie a whole month early, she was ecstatic. She called me two days later to say she read it and was sure the movie rights would go for a bundle. I went to bed that night actually thinking of an idea for my next project. A project I would write completely without the badly dressed little creep and his stupid website. Angela Patterson was ready to start spinning ideas into gold.

One day months later, the publisher called to say they were sending a messenger over with the galley for me to read. All I had to do was look it over, correct it and sign off on it and *City Harmony* would go to press. Within two months, it would be in stores, where Maggie was sure it would debut at Number One.

## It's a Grimm Life

Right after I hung up, there was a knock on the door. Standing there in a lime green hoodie and turquoise sweatpants with a red messenger bag slung over his shoulder was none other than Momus T. Romersklinstill holding an envelope in his hot little hand. Panicking, I looked back toward Trevor's nursery. He was still napping.

"Well, Mrs. Patterson, today's the day," he said, sauntering into my apartment in tie-dyed high top sneakers. "Today's the day we prove you got me to write three books for you. And you know what that means. I get your firstborn son. So, if you just go get the child, you can have this envelope."

I snatched it out of his hands. "Not so fast, troll. You didn't write a third book for me. I did it all by myself. And I can prove it. Yes, it's true, I created a third document from your site."

"Yes," he said. "*The Prince and the Harlot*. Nice try, but I caught it."

"Got a lot of time on your hands, don't you, you little freak? But I scrapped it. It was crap. I wrote *City Harmony* by myself and I'm about to prove it to you."

He looked at me and smiled evilly. "You want to play games? Sure—why not? I have the time. And the winner gets the baby. Fair enough?"

"Sure," I said, as confidently as I could. "I tell you what. I'll give you copies of both manuscripts. And then I'll go make you a nice pot of Lapsang Souchong. Milk and sugar? I'm all out of organic honey."

"Fine," he said.

"You can sit here as long as you want. Compare them. If you can show me anything that leads you to believe *City Harmony* is *The Prince and the Harlot*, you win and the baby's yours."

I went into the kitchen for the pot of tea. I was sure I was going to win, but I was shaking just the same. My son was almost four. Already in nursery school. I'd gone from counting snaps to writing bestsellers. And there was no way I was letting him live under a bridge with a troll in a bad wardrobe. He was mine—just like *City Harmony* was.

When I came back in, Momus was sitting on the couch with two manuscripts spread out in front of him. It seems he'd already printed out a copy of *The Prince and the Harlot* before he came over. He was frantically flipping pages and looking back and forth. I sat the pot of tea on the table.

"Take it away!" he yelled.

"Mr. Romersklinstill, if you wouldn't mind, please be quiet. My son's sleeping."

"Your son? That remains to be seen," he said.

"My son," I said firmly.

He sat there all day long going through the two books. Finally, he swept his hand over the coffee table and scattered pages everywhere. Trevor looked up from his cartoons at the silly man.

"You didn't write this! The devil wrote this! This is not possible!"

I picked up my son. "I win. Time for you to leave."

He let out a scream so loud everything in the apartment shook. Then he pounded his fist on the coffee table. His hand began to vibrate. The vibration worked its way up his arm until his entire body was vibrating. His left eye began to twitch. And then his right. The colors of his clothes began to blend together into swirling patterns. Then he started changing into different outfits. His face began to wink in and out. And then it happened. He started spinning slowly, then faster until he turned into a tornado of multicolored dust and fell to the floor.

"Cool!" Trevor said.

When my husband came home, I'd just finished picking up the papers and vacuuming up the dust. He kissed me on the cheek and picked Trevor up.

"Anything interesting happen today?"

"Same old thing. I wrote, I cleaned, I did some laundry. Trevor napped."

"Boy," he replied. "Your life really is a fairy tale, isn't it?"

WAXWING

by Adrean Messmer

Watching him from her bedroom window always made Juniper feel a little guilty. Kass's curtains were open and framed his room like a stage. The houses were a bit too close together, with just a long, box-cut hedge and a few feet on either side dividing the property. He closed his bedroom door and glanced through his window in her direction, flashing a wicked smile. Juniper ducked, blushing, and turned off her lamp.

Holding onto the sill, she peeked over the top. Kass took off his shirt and tossed it in the corner, flipping his tousled hair out of his eyes. Even in the dim light and even though he knew—more than *knew*, he wanted her to see—she was afraid of getting caught. He stood, with his back to her, pants riding low on his hips and studied the shelf full of DVDs. Settling on one, he put it on and sat on the edge of the bed. She watched as he sped through the beginning of the movie, finally letting it

65

play on a scene of two people, writhing together on a top bunk in what appeared to be a cabin.

He leaned over to the side of the bed and dug something out from under his mattress. Juniper felt her breath get heavy as she watched his muscles and shoulder blades flutter under his skin. In the movie, the woman was on top of the man. Her windswept, eighties hair stayed perfectly in position as her breasts bounced erratically. The camera cut to outside the cabin where a man in a hockey mask slowly climbed the porch steps. The couple didn't notice as he opened the door. The boy ran his hands up the girl's body, stopping to caress her nipples. The man in the mask drew a rusty machete. The girl arched her back, face to the sky, mouth open in ecstasy. The boy dropped his hands to her waist, gripping tightly. The man thrust the machete through the bottom of the mattress, impaling them both in a rush of blood. Placing something in his mouth, Kass's features flickered orange as a lighter's flame danced in his cupped hands.

The sound of Juniper's father's footsteps coming up the stairs startled her back to reality. She managed to yank one of the curtains closed as she jumped into bed and under the covers just before he cracked her door open. His large-shouldered form filled the doorway, blocking all the light. His shadow made her feel cold inside. The only thing missing was the machete.

"Sweetie, are you asleep?"

"No." She gripped the blankets tighter around her, knowing it would buy her time. "I just got to bed."

His silhouette nodded. "Well, get to sleep."

He took a step back into the hallway, stopped, and pushed her door open the rest of the way. Without asking— he never asked— he entered her room.  The rug softened his footfalls as he went to her window.  She sat up to watch him.  Across the way, over the fence, rose bushes, and freshly mown grass, Kass was leaning out his window, looking up at the sky and smoking something that didn't quite look like a cigarette.

Juniper's father shook his head.  His jaw tightened and his dark eyes turned hard as he pulled her curtains closed.  "Stay away from him."

\* \* \* \* \*

She dreamt about her mother, memories long lost to her.  The past slipped away as she awoke with her father's weight on top of her.  When she looked up and it was clear she was awake, he leaned down to her and kissed her on the mouth.

"Go back to sleep, baby."

After he was done, he pulled the blanket tightly around her, tucking her in.  But he left her underwear around her ankles.

\* \* \* \* \*

Two months earlier, Mrs. Christy had caught Juniper in the fourth floor bathroom with a stolen box cutter and blood running down her arms.  The nurse wrapped her arms so tightly, her fingers tingled while she waited for her father to pick her up. Since then, instead of second period gym, she visited the school counselor with five other girls.

One of the girls liked to talk about God, how she was praying and getting better. Kass told Juniper that God never made anything better and she believed him. She couldn't count how many times she'd prayed. She wondered if God even heard her or if he was too busy worrying about more important, godlike things, to notice. Things like how many people were taking his name in vain or the best location for the next natural disaster. Maybe how many children he needed to kill off to meet this quarter's quota. Omniscience meant he knew what she prayed for, before she even asked, and had just decided not to give it to her.

In the hallway after the bell, Kass gave her a wide smile and helped carry her books to her next class. He walked her home too, but he always had to give her stuff back to her at the end of the block. Just in case. On days like this one, when her father's car wasn't in the driveway, he gave her small kisses, leaving the taste of smoke and electric-green soda on her lips.

She went inside, pressing her fingers to her mouth, enjoying the smell of him. Her father stopped her in the foyer, blocking her path. She startled at the sight of him.

"Wh-where's your car?"

He grabbed her small wrist and her books tumbled to the floor. "In the shop. I told you to stay away from him."

"He's just a frie—"

With a jerk, he dragged her up the stairs to her bedroom and threw her on the bed. "You don't kiss friends, you little slut!"

He pulled his belt from the loops as he crossed the room to her. She pushed the hem of her skirt down over her knees. Her curtains were closed. She wished Kass could come through the window and save her. She thought about how Kass's movies always seemed to offer hope even in the darkness moments, a miraculous rebirth out of horrific circumstances. If only...

Juniper's father had forgotten about the grease on his hands and was twisting the rag angrily between his fingers. He watched the house next door. Kass in his upstairs bedroom, disappearing for a moment then reappearing in the living room, gone again, then the sound rumbling as he came around the side of the house, dragging his family's trashcans down the driveway.

Juniper's father remembered looking like that. Young and lean, carelessly disheveled, ready to steal daughters from their fathers and break everybody's heart. He remembered feeling like he could do anything, have anything, be anything. Now his belly, pregnant with liquor and too many TV dinners, weighed him down. Gravity pulled on his skin, making him look old and doughy, fat swelling his large frame. He dropped the rag and went to the edge of his driveway.

"Kass, son. Would you come help me out here?"

The boy set the trash bins by the curb and looked at him uncertainly. "What?"

Juniper's father forced his face into an easy smile. "I need your help. Girls, they're no good at this stuff." He shrugged.

Kass looked at the sky, at Juniper's window, then back to her father. He put his hands on his hips. It looked like he was going to say no. "Just for a minute."

Juniper's father nodded. "It won't take more than that."

* * * * *


His light was on and the curtains were open, but Kass wasn't home.
Juniper watched, brushing her dark hair at the foot of the bed. She waited
until ten o'clock when she heard the hallway creak with her father's weight.
His steps were hurried and she didn't have time to get under the blankets
before he would throw her door open.

But he didn't open the door.

She heard him, heavier than usual, stumbling into the bathroom,
back down the stairs, up and into the bathroom again, grunting and
straining the whole time.

Curiosity was not a virtue. Juniper knew this. Still, she got out of
bed and padded softly to her door. Pressing her ear against it, she listened
to make sure he was busy. She could tell, by the noise, that he'd left the
door open. With a small push, she exited her room and dodged to the other
side of the hallway so he wouldn't be able to see her.

She caught a glimpse of him on his knees, leaning over the side of
the bathtub, rocking back and forth. Slowly as to be silent, she crept
closer. A familiar, acrid smell worked its way into her nose. Closer and
she peered around the doorframe. His arm rose at the elbow, sticky and
red with blood. She stood up, taking two more steps. Closer. Into the
bathroom. The cold of the tile seeped through her thin socks.

Hot tears blurred her vision. She thought about the walk home.
Kass's kiss. Off-brand green soda. Lunchtime and him picking French
fries off her plate. She thought about watching him through her window.
She thought about anything but him lying in the tub. Anything but how his

hands were no longer where they belonged. Anything but the blood all around him.

She lunged at her father. "Stop it! What are you doing?"

He grabbed her arm and pulled her around in front of him and, with his hand over hers, he forced her fingers around the knife. He guided her hand down, into Kass's cooling flesh. The blood didn't pour or pump. It oozed slowly and thickly, like cement. Chunks of it already coagulated.

"I said to stay away. You couldn't just stay away."

Juniper gagged and looked away. Apologies begged to be said aloud, but she was afraid of her father so she thought them. She thought them as loudly as she could and hoped Kass could hear. It felt like she was there for days, with her father behind her, holding her close. Her heart beat to the rhythm of the cutting.

They filled up three trash bags.

Before he let her go, her father whispered into her ear hotly, "Now you're a part of this." He stood up. The sweat that had built up between them cooled quickly. He left the bags in the bathroom, blood pooling around them.

\* \* \* \* \*

She couldn't sleep. She kept thinking about Kass alone on the cold tile of the bathroom. She thought about the movies he watched. She never got the sound, but they were blood-soaked, full of people dying and, miraculously, coming back. Clawing their way through the dirt back to the starlit night.

71

## It's a Grimm Life

She slipped out of bed to the bathroom.  The bags still sat in the middle of the floor, the puddles around them brown and sticky.  One by one, she cradled him in her arms as she carried them—him— down and out to the backyard.  He was heavier than she expected, but dragging would have left trails on the carpet.  She leaned on the wall to keep from falling down the stairs.

The warm, sweet smell of the evergreens filled her senses.  Small, blue, hard berries littered the ground around the tree she set the bags under.  The shovel was in the garage and Juniper had to sneak through the side door to get it.  By the time she finished burying him, the sky was turning pale gold and birds had started to sing.  Her back ached and blisters had formed and popped on her hands.  She left the shovel by the fresh earth and went inside.

She cringed as her father patted her shoulder.  "Go take a shower, baby."

\* \* \* \* \*

She spent the day in the nurse's office, feigning general malaise.  The nurse smiled at her sweetly, asked about Aunt Flo, and let her sleep most of the day.  Juniper woke only when the bells echoed through the halls.

The walk home was long.  She stopped on the sidewalk in front of Kass's house.  Even in the bright afternoon, she thought she could see his light still on.  She followed the path of syncopated stones through the grass up to the front door.  Three knocks and then rushed footsteps.  His mother opened the door. Her eyes were red, like she'd been up all night, but she smiled.

"Hey, sweetie." She invited Juniper inside. "Have you seen Kass?"

Surprised at how easily the lie came, like it had been waiting behind her teeth to jump out and attack, she said, "No. I thought he was sick, so I came to see him." Then, feeling like it was unfinished, she added, "He isn't here?"

His mother shook her head. "I called the police, but they say he's just being a teenager." She smiled tensely. "He'll be home soon, I'm sure."

Juniper nodded. "Uh, is it okay if I leave his homework in his room?"

"Yeah, of course. He'll need it."

She stayed at the bottom of the stairs, watching the front door, the ragged nail of her index finger pinched between her top and bottom teeth.

In Kass's room, Juniper let her hand run over the soft wood of his desk, skewing the papers scattered on it, as she stepped carefully over the piles of clothes and stuff covering the floor. She'd never been inside his room before, only caught glimpses from her bedroom window. He'd moved in the year before and caught her watching him unpack. He'd stopped and written "HI" in thick black letters on the side of a box and held it up to the window. It was tradition after that. Every morning, after he'd hit his snooze button a dozen times, he'd roll off the bed, hair messy and wrinkled clothes, and hold up the sign for her. It was still there, ragged edges and bent corners.

She sat at the edge of his bed, taking in his smell, feeling surrounded by him. He'd filled every available space. The walls were covered in posters and pages torn from horror magazines. Girls in shredded clothes, covered in blood. Guys turning into monsters. Hordes of undead staring hungrily from their glossy prisons. The patchwork wallpaper was broken only by five wall-mounted shelves holding his movie collection.

She bent down and picked up one of his t-shirts, a white one with an intricate sugar skull on the front, and pulled it over her grey dress. She went to the shelves and ran her finger along the spines. She'd seen so many from her window. She knew which ones to look for. She pulled a few down and sat on the floor, fast forwarding to right before the action started.

That night at dinner, Juniper couldn't eat. She kept her palms pressed against the table, feeling her shivers go all the way down through the legs, setting the ground trembling. She was sure the whole neighborhood could feel it. She thought about Kass in the ground, his bones rattling together in the damp, dark hole. She couldn't look at her father. His voice came through, muddled and incomprehensible. Finally, he took her plate away and she went upstairs.

By eleven-thirty, she'd heard him go to bed. Down in the kitchen, she took the sharpest knife she could find in the drawer, testing each blade on the tips of her fingers.

The night air was cool, raising goose bumps on her skin. In the branches above the disturbed earth, she saw a flash of yellow in the dim light from the lamppost in the neighbor's yard. The tail feathers of a waxwing, probably.

With a deep breath, she drew the knife across her palm and watched the blood drip onto the dirt.

"Faithful lover, six feet down. Hear your name above the ground. Return to me safe and sound. Assurgi mortuus et capessito ultionis tuum."

She prayed that it would work. Kass's movies had different ways of doing it, different incantations, different components. Not knowing where to begin, she cobbled together her own script with what little she caught from film, bound together with desperation and dread.

She waited to hear the earth stir. For Kass's hand to reach up to her. For the sky to darken. Clouds to cover a full, red moon and blot out the stars. But nothing happened. She sat down and leaned against the rough bark of the tree. Above her, the bird twitched its wings, shaking the leaves.

She woke up to its song as the sun shot rays of red through the murky blue sky. Her father's figure filled the back door. She scrambled to her tingling feet and went inside for breakfast.

They were both quiet as he served her eggs and buttered the toast. A soft tapping on the window broke the silence. She looked up to see a small grey and yellow bird. It—no, he. She wasn't sure how she knew, but somehow she just *knew* it was a male. He tapped on the glass again. The sound was clear and rang like a bell, louder each time. Her father followed her gaze. The waxwing bounced from one side of the sill to the other, tapping along the way, as if searching for a weak spot.

Without thinking about it, Juniper stood up, knocking her chair over, and went to the sink. The bird cocked his head. His eyes were green, she realized, like Kass's. She pushed the window open and he fluttered up to her hand. The smile didn't finish forming on her lips before her father's shadow fell over her. He snagged the hand towel and lashed at the bird.

The bird fell with a thud to the counter. Looking dazed, he jumped unsteadily back to his feet. As he did, another waxwing landed on the window ledge. Then another. And another. They filled the sill and poured inside, tumbling over each other, taking up space on the counter, in the sink.

Juniper cupped the green-eyed bird in her hands and dove under the table. The room darkened as the others took flight, a storm cloud of beating wings. They circled the room, swirling around her father. Something wet splashed against her face. She touched it and her fingers came away red. Peering through the tornado of feathers, she saw her father batting at the birds. One dove at him, and his left eye burst in a clear and bloody splash. He put his arms up to shield himself, but they pecked at him, puncturing skin and pulling on tendons. She let the bird in her hand drop into her lap and covered her ears against the sound of beating wings and screaming.

Then, one by one, the birds left, out the same window. Running down the cabinets, she saw her father. Dark pieces of him, the size of stew meat, soaked in red broth, dripping on the floor. His clothes were shredded, floating like dust in the air.

Juniper looked down at the bird still perched on her skirt. He looked up at her, a fine mist of blood coating his feathers. When she put her hand near him, he nuzzled into it.

"I'm sorry," she whispered.

He sang to her again. The same song he'd woken her with.

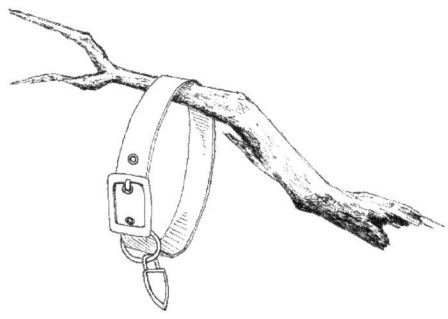

## THE NATURE OF SOME BEASTS

### by T. S. Kummelman

Only a few days into their friendship, The Dog looked upon The Cat who was sitting on her rock, and a thought occurred to him, one he hadn't had before. This perplexed him so that he stared off in the distance, his head cocked to the side.

The Cat saw The Dog thusly, studied him for a moment, then turned away, writing it off as another instance of his stupidity.

When The Dog had stayed in the same position long enough for a squirrel to have crept slowly past them in the small clearing, catching the curious eye of the feline, but never once that of the usually hyper canine, The Cat looked in the same direction. Seeing nothing but the chuckling brook and the reeds which grew upon its banks, she set her head back down again and sighed.

She became drowsy, wondering whether he had had a sudden brain injury and would never move again. The only time he ever stayed so long in one pose was when he was sleeping, and even that would be interrupted by his stupid paws suddenly freaking out of their own accord in some stupid dream run. It could be time to rid herself of this one.

Just as the eyes of The Cat were drifting closed, she realized The Idiot still had not moved, not so much as to twitch his tail. She bolted upright, looking about for danger. Finding none, she approached The Dog, and swatted at his stupid head to break his reverie. The swat was hard enough that it made the metal tags on his collar jingle.

The Dog looked shocked, and scampered back from his obviously annoyed companion. Why would you do that, he asked. He'd been deep in thought, and, so far as he knew, had done nothing to offend The Cat.

You were bothering me, The Cat answered.

All I was doing was pondering a thought, he said. For that, you strike me?

You? The Cat looked aghast, which was no easy feat for an animal whose face is covered with fur. A thought?! And pondering, at that! Who gave you leave to think?

Now it was The Dog's turn to look aghast, which is easy for a dog, as they use more facial muscles than cats, who mainly use their faces to express annoyance and anger—and it just so happens to be the same expression for both. I have a brain, he said. How could I not think?

The Cat chuckled, although her face still looked annoyed. Your brain functions on four levels: sleep, eat, chase squirrels, and hump. Whereas mine own works on levels you could never comprehend.

The Dog looked down at the grass, ashamed. Then, he turned away.

The Cat stared at him for a moment, then, realizing she had hurt his feelings, nuzzled up against him. Surely this is no surprise to you, she said. It is nothing of which to be ashamed. You are a dog, it is your nature. I am a cat, I have many natures.

Tell me, The Cat said, trying her best to sound interested, which she was not, of course—but she knew if they did not settle this, it would bother her for the remainder of the afternoon and interrupt her napping. What was your thought?

The Dog was silent for a moment, then looked back at her.

I was wondering why you should be the smarter one, he answered. Why is it I am doomed to be the clumsy one? Why is it I must be the butt of your jokes? I am larger than you, and my brain, naturally, should be larger as well. Therefore, I should be the smarter one.

**It's a Grimm Life**

The Cat was silent for a moment, then began shaking her head.

What is it, The Dog asked.

Over there, she said, motioning to the base of a tree not twenty feet away. She saw The Dog look in that direction, his ears perked forward, and before his eyes adjusted to the shady gloom there, she yelled SQUIRREL!

The Dog took off like an angry hornet, straight at the tree. That settled, she climbed back up to her rock and laid down to nap.

* * * * *

The Squirrel's only job was to lead The Dog to the overpass.

This may sound like an easy task, but the overpass was no short distance away, and The Squirrel was smaller than The Dog, so it was basically running five hundred miles to The Dog's one. The trick was to keep The Dog's attention while it rested between bursts of running; its favorite method was to sit in the lower branches of a tree and throw things at him.

The Squirrel, unlike The Cat, was angry most of the time. Whereas The Cat cared about nothing besides eating, napping, and tormenting The Dog, everything pissed off The Squirrel. When he did stop for rests, he had to constantly remind himself to keep the mad chattering to a minimum, lest he wind himself from yelling at the overgrown hairball. Yet there was also

The Cat's promise at the back of his mind: lead The Dog to the overpass, and The Cat would not eat him.

A fair enough arrangement, were you to ask The Squirrel.

\* \* \* \* \*

Ten minutes later, The Dog was walking along the embankment, frazzled, disappointed, a little wet from a spill he took in the creek, and very upset with The Cat.

He knew, deep down, that his chances of ever catching the squirrels were, at best, remote. He blamed it not on his ability to hunt, but rather on the tags that hung from his collar, which jangled incessantly whenever he gave chase. He was doomed to ever chase them, never catching, because they could hear him coming.

Not recognizing where he was now, he walked a little further, where the creek widened and became a stream. He saw a deer on the other side, drinking, but it paid him no mind, for it knew before he was halfway across it could scamper up the opposite embankment and be gone.

Soon The Dog came upon a concrete bridge. He caught the scent of something rotten beneath it, and as his eyes adjusted, he saw a big shape under there, hiding in the shadows. He sniffed the air again, snorted and sniffed, and let out an inquisitive bark. What was under the bridge was big, and smelled kind of bad.

Please, came a voice, I am hungry.

The Dog cocked his head to the side. Who are you?

I am but a poor, hungry thing, said the voice. Shunned by all, loved by none.

Then why don't you come out and eat something, The Dog inquired. Squirrels are delicious, if you can catch them before they run up a tree, and so long as you are not wearing a noisy collar. He sat, not daring to draw nearer. The voice sounded weak enough, but if the big thing was hungry, he would rather not take his chances. I may be stupid like The Cat says, he thought, but I am no idiot.

Because the sun would kill me, came the voice from under the bridge. Could you not bring me something to eat?

That was when it dawned on The Dog, and he smiled. I know what you are, he said. You are The Troll, and as soon as I get close enough, you will snatch me up and eat me.

The Troll seemed to shudder in the darkness. Heavens no, it said. I would never eat a dog. The meat is too stringy, and the fur too soft. Nothing personal, you understand.

No offense taken, The Dog answered. But why didn't you eat more last night, when the sun wasn't out?

Oh, I had plenty to eat, answered The Troll. I was just looking for a little snack. You see, I suffer from IBS.

The Dog cocked his head to the side, puzzling over the reference. When it dawned on him what The Troll meant, his tail began to wag in self-congratulations.

Oh, he proclaimed, you have Irritable Bowel Syndrome.

If only, The Troll responded, shaking his head sadly. I have Inconsistent Bowel Syndrome. The extra fiber helps clear things out.

Ah, said The Dog. Oh. Well. Glad I could help? And what is it you like to eat, he asked.

When The Troll answered him, The Dog thought for a moment and grinned. I have just the thing, he said, and bounded back the way he had come.

\* \* \* \* \*

### It's a Grimm Life

It's just up ahead, he told The Cat.

The curious, curious cat. Who at first had thought The Dog to be lying, but his excitement over finding what he called a "flock of humans", which were always easy for a free meal, had seemed exuberant.

Where are they, The Cat asked, seeing no trace of any humans. She saw no cars, no picnics, not even any of the trash they often left behind.

Under the bridge, sheltering from the heat of the day. The Dog trotted towards the underneath, dark part of the bridge, his tail wagging stupidly.

Wait, said The Cat. You know I should go first, for I am the cuter of the two, and they will warm up to my attention better than to yours.

The Dog stopped for a moment, looking back at The Cat. What do you mean, you are the cuter one? I can do tricks and fetch things, and they like me better because I make them laugh.

Actually, said The Cat, catching up to The Dog, they are laughing at you. They marvel at how stupid you are, that you would run off and bring back something they threw away. I should go first, as I am cuter. And smarter.

The Dog bristled at this, and let out a low growl.

Then why do they always seem happy to see that I have brought the stick back to them?

The Cat stopped and looked up at him. They humor you because they feel sorry for your stupidity. Which is why I should go first.

The Dog hesitated for a moment, then bounded ahead of The Cat, leaping forward and into the darkness. I'll show you who the dumb one is, he cried, but The Cat had stopped following and sat looking into the darkness. Just as a large truck passed overhead, there came from under the bridge a yelp, then a rather loud crunching sound.

After a few moments of crunching, then a great gulp, came a contented sigh.

Thank you again, Cat, said The Troll. Same thing next week?

Probably, said The Cat. Dogs are the easiest.

A human would be nice, once in a while.

They are harder to trick, answered The Cat. But we shall see.

With that, The Cat wandered off to find a new victim, carrying away with it the fish The Troll had tossed to it. Once she got back to her rock and began to eat the fish, she pondered the stupidity of dogs. And squirrels, which, like birds, were never far from her mind.

\* \* \* \* \*

**It's a Grimm Life**

Under the bridge, The Troll stroked The Dog's fur with one giant finger.

You should probably run along now, he said to The Dog.

The Dog looked at The Troll before gazing up and beyond the overpass, in the direction the road lay. Did the tree branches hurt your teeth, he asked, motioning down at the remaining pile of twigs and fallen branches he had fetched for The Troll earlier.

The Troll chuckled. Not at all. I prefer eating wood over flesh.

But you are a troll ... I thought all trolls ate humans and animals and such.

That, said The Troll, is an unfounded assumption. Much like how The Cat mistakes your attention deficiency for lack of intelligence, everyone assumes that since I am large and on the rather unattractive side, I eat everything that moves. Which I do not.

He thought for a moment, then looked back at the gentle giant. But hasn't the cat brought other dogs this way? Why was it you helped me, and ate the others?

The Troll stared at The Dog, his mouth agape. Do you see any bones lying about?

The Dog inspected the closest thing which he had mistaken for a bone, and realized, now that he was close to it, that it was just bits of tree, stripped of bark, laid bare to the pale wood beneath.

I keep scraps about so The Cat will hear me crunching on something.

So you let them all go?

Of course. Do you not see how this works? The Cat brings me dogs, who fetch sticks and branches for me to eat. I give The Cat the fish I catch under this bridge so that she will keep bringing dogs to me. And then I show you another path to take, which could lead you to better company. See, we all have our lots in life. It is up to you how you play your role, just as it is up to you how you allow others to perceive you. Do you see now?

The one piece of information The Troll kept to himself was that of The Squirrel's role in the whole affair; he saw no sense in ruining The Dog's love of chasing the fuzzy little rodents—not to mention the fact that trying to explain conspiracies to dogs was like trying to teach a cat to smile.

The Dog thought about it for a moment. You are much better company than she, he finally answered. Come to think of it, I am smarter than The Cat, aren't I? Because The Stupid Cat never once thought that a bridge would be there because of a road, and a road leads away from the bridge, and to humans, and to food. And shelter. And family.

The Troll sighed. You are right there, my friend. Before you go, however, allow me to do one last favor for you. You will have to trust me, and lean forward a bit....

## It's a Grimm Life

The Dog did as he was asked, looking down at the ground. With two large fingers, The Troll managed to unlatch the collar, and tossed it in a pile where several others lay.

That should make it easier to hunt the squirrels, don't you think? Now run along. Night will be here soon, and you can seek better shelter than under this dark, dank bridge.

After saying goodbye with another friendly lick upon The Troll's massive hand, The Dog trotted away, tail wagging, down the road which would lead him to anywhere, anywhere away from The Cat.

\* \* \* \* \*

Although twenty minutes later, his new journey was nearly jeopardized when a squirrel ran across the road.

But it only took him an hour to find the road again, which The Dog took as a marked improvement.

KURT & WOLFGANG'S FINAL SHOW

by Victor Hyde

Last night Kurt thought about swallowing two dozen painkillers and sleeping forever. But the thought of leaving Wolfgang behind had stopped him. Now in light of morning, he doesn't want to die—he just wants to drink.

"It's going to be okay," says Kurt. "We'll find another gig. You'll be okay. Me too. Even if we lose this place, then we just find another one."

Wolfgang just stares out in front of him, not looking at Kurt.

"I know people that owe me favors. Some even owe me money."

Those were lies, of course. Kurt knows he's not fooling Wolfgang. After thirty years there are no secrets between them.

Kurt sucks down the last swills of tepid beer. It makes him wince but he is already getting up from the couch to fetch another.

"You want?" he asks Wolfgang. Wolfgang doesn't answer.

"Come on, man. This affects me as well," he says. There's desperation in his eyes as he waits for Wolfgang to say something, anything. There's nothing.

It's just after 9AM when Kurt takes out his fifth beer of the day. He bangs it against the counter. The bottle cap pops off and spins like a golden coin. The beer tastes like real treasure.

The apartment looks like a college dorm the morning after a party. A stack of pizza boxes decorated with coagulated cheese and orange cheese curl crumbs takes over an entire seat of the couch. Fifteen bottles of beer, green bottles as well as amber bottles (Kurt is an equal opportunity drinker) stand in a skew formation next to Kurt's favorite recliner. The coffee table is covered in cigarette ash and marked with the water rings of beer bottles that had fallen in the binge.

Kurt falls into the recliner and turns up the TV. His head has been aching for thirty-two hours straight and the shrill sound of the TV stabs at him. He grits his teeth, takes another swallow of beer and lets it all just flow. He feels Wolfgang staring at him.

"What is it?" he asks.

"Nothing," Wolfgang mumbles.

"It's never nothing. It's always something. Talk to me."

"It sucks the fat one just sitting here," says Wolfgang. "Maybe you can find an office job and start providing."

"You'd like that!" says Kurt. "So you can just sit in a dark closet the whole day."

Wolfgang doesn't offer anything else and Kurt turns back to the TV. He can't follow the cartoon. A yellow dog keeps growing longer legs and a boy in a white panda hat swings around a sword. *This* is what kids want. That is why he is sitting here in the middle of the week drinking beer and why Wolfgang is sitting over there slumped in self-pity.

"Pathetic," Wolfgang says.

"Excuse me."

"You heard me. Pathetic. All of this. You. You are pathetic."

Kurt finishes the beer and chucks the bottle at Wolfgang. It hits him in the chest, bounces off and rolls over the stained carpet.

"Fuck you," says Kurt and he is surprised at the amount of anger he feels. Wolfgang just stares out in front of him.

To fuel the angry monster inside him, Kurt digs his fingers into the back of the recliner and pulls out a crumpled piece of paper. Two days ago it was white and formal, now it is blending in nicely with its surroundings. It's full of *THANK YOU*s and *MANY YEARS OF SERVICE* and words like *FAITHFUL* and *CONTRIBUTION* and *GOOD SPIRIT*. Empty words because the letter only served to tell him that he no longer had a job. Correction. That he *and* Wolfgang no longer had a job. First time in thirty years without a job. It's the last time he is reading it. He scrunches it up and tosses it at Wolfgang.

The piece of paper catches a corner of the Tower of Pizza and it collapses on top of Wolfgang, burying him in a heap of boxes. Kurt is on his feet immediately to pull Wolfgang from the rubble. He dusts off the cheese crumbs from Wolfgang's fur.

"I'm sorry," says Kurt. "I don't know what else to say. I'm too old. You're too old. But we will find something else. They don't know what they've lost."

Wolfgang snorts.

"*You're* too old, Kurtie, Auntie Girty," says Wolfgang. His voice is two parts Bela Lugosi and three parts the Count from "Sesame Street".

The phone rings. Kurt looks at Wolfgang. Wolfgang looks at Kurt. They go answer it together. Kurt just knows it's *Entertainco* with an apology. He rips the phone from its cradle.

"It's Kurt. How can I help?" He is surprised to hear the slur in his voice.

"Kurt, it's John Butch here. I've had complaints from the neighbors about noise levels from your apartment."

It takes Kurt a second to start impersonating the voice of one of the cashiers at the 7-Eleven. It comes out girlish and sweet, flawlessly accurate in spite of his inebriation.

"I'm sorry—Mr. Butch you said your name was? —but Kurt is not here at the moment."

"Cut the crap, Kurt. You told me it was you talking."

A pause.

"Listen, I'm not making a noise. I'm just watching TV."

"Really? Because it sounds to me like you need to shout to hear yourself."

"Fine. I'll turn it down."

Kurt slams the phone back in its cradle.

"What a dick," says Wolfgang.

Kurt detours to the kitchen and gets another beer. He puts Wolfgang on the table so that he can open the bottle. Wolfgang grumbles about how only dishes are put on tables. By the time Kurt gets back to the couch, he has already forgotten about the call.

There's a different cartoon on TV. *Dexter's Laboratory.* A pointless show. What kid wants his cartoons so serious?

Wolfgang throws his head back and howls, "Boy, this is nooooo good!"

Five minutes later the telephone rings again. It must be *Entertainco* calling to apologize. They were wrong. The cocksure kid with the talking skeleton (have you ever heard of such a ridiculous thing?) was no replacement for Kurt and Wolfgang. Kurt gets the children to laugh and Wolfgang gets the children to love.

He answers in Clint Eastwood's voice.

"Yes? Can I help?"

The person on the other end sighs.

"Just cut the bullshit, Kurt. I'm in no mood," says John.

"Kurt's not here at the mo..."

"I told you to mind the neighbors. Get your act together or I'm taking this further."

"Fine."

"No, it's not *fine*. I don't know what you've been doing the last few days but it's getting out of hand. You don't want me to start throwing the building's rules at you. I might just decide that it's time to kick your sorry ass out. You're late on rent. Again."

Kurt doesn't answer. He stares at Wolfgang and Wolfgang stares at him.

"Kurt!"

"Yeah, all right. I'm turning it off. Relax."

He puts the phone back in the cradle, gently this time. He mutes the TV and finishes his beer. Something burns inside him.

"You know what you have to do, right?" Wolfgang asks.

Kurt nods.

His T-shirt has a yellow stain on it from when he vomited on himself the night before. He hides it by pulling on a jacket. It's Day Three for the shorts but they still seem fine. He puts on his shoes. As he stands up he notices himself in the mirror against the wall. A fat, red face with a pubic hair beard. There are clumps of gel in his hair.

He lifts Wolfgang up to take a look. Wolfgang's orange fur looks dirty and matted and a far cry from the plush, shiny curls he wore on stage. Wolfgang has bags under his eyes, a black nub of a nose, long fingers and black claws. Wolfgang often tells the kids: "I'm so ugly, I'm beautiful."

Kurt opens the door and steps into the passage. He closes his apartment's door softly behind him.

He puts his ear against his neighbor's door and listens. Nothing. He goes to the next apartment. Also nothing. At the third apartment he hears the clink of a spoon in a teacup and someone clearing their throat. It's that old bitch, Mrs. Roberts. Laura. Wolfgang is still on his right hand so Kurt uses his left to knock.

"Coming!"

Kurt puts a finger over the peephole.

A shadow appears under the door and the door rattles in its frame as Laura pushes up against it to peek into the corridor.

"Who is it?"

"It's John Butch," Kurt says in the caretaker's voice.

"Hold on."

A key turns and a security chain rattles against the door. Mrs. Roberts opens the door wide. She's wearing a dress that could have been a curtain once; purple floral print with white lace trim around the neck and a string of yellowed imitation pearls. Her hair is like wool and tinted purple, still flat on the side where she slept.

"John?"

"Afraid not."

"What do you want? Where's John?"

"I don't know where John is. How are you, Laura?"

She looks down at Wolfgang on Kurt's right hand.

"I ... I am fine," she says.

Her face is deeply lined. Her pursed lips create lines from the corner of her mouth to her chin, like a ventriloquist's puppet. Only this is one puppet Kurt wouldn't put his hand up in.

"Good," says Kurt. "Listen, I'm sorry about the noise."

A pause. Laura nods.

"It's fine. Sorry I had to call John."

"Oh, so *you* called him?"

Laura's eyes widen and she reaches for the door to slam it shut. Kurt puts his foot in the way.

"Go away! I have nothing to say to you."

"Oh, you had plenty to say *about* me."

"John!" Laura cries.

"John!" Wolfgang imitates perfectly.

Kurt shoulders the door. It bashes into Laura's face and she stumbles backwards. Blood the color of oil pours from her forehead and down her nose. She opens her mouth to scream and Kurt rushes his hand up to silence her, instead knocking her hard between the eyes. Her eyes roll back and she falls over, hits her head against the coffee table and she's out.

Kurt stands over her, chest heaving. The last five seconds are a blur. Somehow he feels violated. His mouth is dry. He looks at the throbbing knuckles of his left hand and thanks God he wore Wolfgang on the right otherwise he would have really socked her one. The thought loosens a chuckle but before it can turn into laughter, he sees the blood on the tablecloth and the puddle of it growing beneath her head. The alcohol drains from his system and leaves him with a cold, clay ball in the pit of his stomach.

Kurt listens but all is quiet. He closes the door and locks it, dropping the key into his pocket.

The couch is so worn he feels its wooden frame as he sits down. There's a lot of knitted and lacy items throughout the apartment. One of the walls has been turned into the inevitable album, with peeling photos stuck to the wall, the black and white ones from her youth in expensive frames from when having pictures taken was still a proper affair. The air smells of vitamins and something else, both sweet and rotten. There is a tissue holder on the coffee table that is nothing more than a two liter Coke bottle that's been cut open and dressed in a pig outfit, knitted by the lady on the floor.

Laura looks dead.

Shit.

Kurt takes a deep breath and puts two fingers against her turkey flap neck. It takes him almost a minute to locate a pulse. It's faint and fast. He doesn't know what it means but he guesses the old bird is on her way out.

He falls back onto the couch. He looks at Wolfgang. Wolfgang looks at him.

"Take her to the bathroom," says Wolfgang. "That's where we take our messes. Especially little accidents."

"And then?"

"Then you pack your suitcase and wave goodbye. When the oinkers get here and they find this old lady up in Heaven, they're going to ask questions. How many places did you leave your fingerprints? Better make it look like the old girl had a slip in the bath."

Sometimes Wolfgang speaks a lot of sense. Kurt's going to need two hands for this. He props Wolfgang up on the couch—*you rest,* he says—and gets to work.

Kurt grabs the old lady under the armpits and drags her to the bathroom. She's heavy, like a large bag of compost. Smells like she shat herself. Her head flops back against him. He feels warm blood soaking through his shorts.

The bathroom is small and old. Kurt dumps Laura in the bath. Her dress hikes up and shows knees like apricot pits and a network of varicose veins. Her feet with thick, yellowed toenails dangle over the side of the bath. Both her slippers must have fallen off in the process.

Kurt uses towels and the bathmat to clean up the blood in the living room.

"Better do a good job," says Wolfgang.

He does.

A knock on the door.

Kurt's heart beats in his ears. He doesn't move, scared to make a sound.

Another knock, more insistent.

"Gran'ma! It's Kelly. I got your food and medicine."

His spit dries up. That was the voice of a teenager. If she brought medicine, it means she expected Laura to be home.

"It's a good thing," Wolfgang whispers. "Old ladies on drugs can easily fall over in the bath."

Kurt glares at Wolfgang and mashes a finger to his lips.

"Gran'ma, I'm coming in."

The doorknob turns but of course it is locked. The key is in Kurt's pocket. Kurt grins at the door and the hapless child on the other side. He gives Wolfgang a thumbs up.

Then he hears the jingle of keys and Kurt goes cold. A key slides into the lock with a click. Kurt sees the security chain hanging unfastened. It would stop her. He takes a step in that direction but hears the lock clack open. He turns and bolts for the bathroom, remembering at the last second to scoop up the bloody towels.

"Gran'ma, I'm coming in. Final warning."

Courteous little cunt.

The apartment door creaks open just as Kurt slips into the bathroom. He closes the bathroom door. He reaches for the key to lock the bathroom. There isn't one.

*Fuck!*

"Gran'ma, are you okay?"

He listens to Kelly walking through the apartment.

A knock on the bathroom door.

"Gran'ma?"

Kurt has no choice. If he doesn't answer she's going to try the door.

"Yes?" he answers in Laura's voice. He adds a sickly croak to it.

"Oh, thank God," says Kelly. "I didn't know where you were. I thought ... Didn't you hear me calling?"

"No, sorry. The water was running."

"I brought you your medicine."

"Thank you."

"And some cream donuts."

"Oh, that's lovely."

"Are you okay, Gran'ma? You don't sound well."

Kurt imitates a cough.

"I'm fine, fine. Just taking a quick bath. You can leave the medicine at the door and come back later. I'm going to be a while."

"It's okay," says Kelly. "I don't mind waiting. I brought myself a cream donut as well. We can eat together."

Footsteps moving away from the bathroom door. Kurt puts his hands over his eyes and tries to count to ten. Then he remembers the blood on the tablecloth and Wolfgang still sitting on the couch. How well did he clean up?

He hears a squeak and the groan of the apartment's ancient pipes. Kelly is fetching herself a glass of water. There's a rattle he recognizes as a bottle of pills.

"Sure is a lot of pills," says Kelly.

Kurt decides not to answer even though Wolfgang is dying to say *Pills and chills for ladies over the hills.* Kurt worries about him.

Kurt puts his eye to the keyhole. From here he can only see one end of the couch and the coffee table but it's the end that matters. Wolfgang is propped up in the corner of the couch looking both terrified and angry. Kurt winks at him even though he knows Wolfgang won't be able to see it through the keyhole.

Kelly steps into view. She's wearing jeans and a red hoodie that says LIFEGUARD in bold white letters. Clearly it is store bought because Kelly could only serve as a lifeguard if her very round body doubles as a raft. Her hair is pulled into a tight ponytail which was a bad move because she doesn't have the skin for it. Kurt guesses she's sixteen.

She has a jug-sized glass of water in her hand. A body that size must need a lot of fluids. She stops when she sees Wolfgang and for a few long seconds they simply stare at each other.

"Hallo," says Kelly but Wolfgang doesn't reply; he doesn't like fat children.

She reaches out slowly as if she is scared that Wolfgang would bite her. It's silly—Wolfgang would never bite children. She touches his chest and his tail, rubbing the orange-brown fur between her fingers. She grimaces. Kurt feels a dark wash of anger as she wipes her hand on her jeans.

She turns to put the glass on the coffee table and that's when she sees the blood. She reaches out a fat finger—clearly this girl cannot make up her mind about something unless she's touched it. She smells her fingertip and rubs her thumb and finger together. Kurt notices she doesn't wipe her hand.

"What happened here?" she calls. Kurt doesn't answer.

She walks to the bathroom. Kurt stands up and grips the doorknob tightly.

"Gran'ma? What happened? Why is there blood on the table?"

He can't ignore her now.

"Oh, *that,*" he says. "My nose started bleeding. It was nothing."

"Are you sure you're okay?"

"Yes yes, really," says Kurt. "I'm going to be a while. You should really go home. I'll call you when I'm feeling better."

"Are you chasing me away?" Kelly asks playfully.

Careful now.

"Of course not," says Kurt, "but I really think it's better."

"Well, I'm not going. I want to see you for myself."

He sighs dramatically, hard enough for her to hear. He wishes he had the strength to punch her right through the door.

"What doll is that?"

"Doll? What doll?"

"The dog-thing on the couch."

"Oh, *that*. It's a wolf, can't you see?"

*Are you blind?*

"It's actually an antique. Cool, isn't it?"

Kelly snorts like a happy pig.

"Did you just say 'cool'?"

Fuck. He did.

"Just trying to fit in."

He feels cold sweat on his brow.

"Ha," says Kelly. "That's cool. But the wolf is pretty freaky looking."

Kurt wonders how she can't feel Wolfgang's eyes boring into her back—he can feel it right through the door.

"I don't know what that means."

"I mean it looks funny. Like a retarded baby in a dog's costume."

"Oh," says Kurt. "I don't see it like that."

*Please don't say anything, Wolfgang. Take a deep breath and stay calm.*

"Mind if I watch some TV?"

"Sure," says Kurt and as the tension breaks he feels exhaustion wash through him.

He watches her walk away. She takes a seat on the other end of the couch, away from Wolfgang, where he can't see her. The TV clicks on and he hears it flick through a news report, Wimbledon commentary and a wildlife show before settling on some daytime soap. At least it's not *Dexter's Laboratory*.

Kurt looks around the bathroom. There's a small window above the bath, big enough to let light in and steam out, but it would be a very tight fit for Kurt. It's three floors up and Kurt doesn't know what's on the other side.

Above the stained basin is a mirrored bathroom cabinet. He opens it. Inside is a toothbrush with frayed and flared bristles. There's a glass filled with murky water where Laura must keep her dentures. He finds a cucumber face mask in a sealed foil packet, the model posing on it has sliced cucumbers on her eyes and her mouth open like she's so fucking ecstatic about the face mask she can't contain herself. Above the bath, there's a pink shower cap hanging from the ancient shower head.

The blood has soaked into Laura's hair. She looks like she's wearing a cap of afterbirth. Her breath makes small burring sounds in the back of her throat.

Kurt paces the bathroom which means taking one step towards the door, turning, and taking one step towards the bath. Outside a man says, "Gloria! How could you? He's my son!" Kelly giggles.

Kurt looks at Laura's wrinkled knees, the granadilla-skin face. He looks at a woman that's thumbing the doorbell at Death's mansion. If he goes out now and tells Kelly, they can still save her. It would be over for Kurt but it would be better than if they caught him after she died.

WWWD?

What would Wolfgang do?

*I'm thinking Mrs. Doubtfire.*

Kurt compares Laura's body shape to his. Her dress is as shapeless as her body. Kurt wonders if he could do it.

*You're not one of the best impersonators on the planet for nothing,* Wolfgang thinks but Kurt hears it as if it's his own thought.

Her feet are so bloated they look inflated. He pushes them into the bath. *Thunk thunk.* Then he reaches down and hikes her dress up above her hips. She's wearing cream-colored underwear, giant-sized. Her skin is pale and spotted, with pink sores spotted all over her stomach. Kurt swallows and swallows to keep the sick down. He lifts her by the armpits so that she sits up. A low moan escapes her and he bunches up a fist in case it gets louder. Luckily he doesn't have to use it. He pulls hard and the dress comes up over her head. The effort snaps the string of fake pearls and they go flying, pattering into the bath. He lets go of Laura and she slumps back, hitting her head against the faucet. She lets out a deep sigh.

There's blood on the back of the dress but he will just have to make sure that he doesn't show Kelly that side. He strips down. He takes a deep breath, scrunches up his nose and starts worming himself into the dress. It's loose around him and smells like sweet mothballs. It will have to do.

The legs sticking from the dress belong to a gorilla. Wolfgang would snicker at the sight. Luckily there's the razor. He runs water into the basin, grabs the razor and gets to work. Dry shaving is the worst and he nicks himself. Outside, the show ends.

"Still okay, Gran'ma?"

"Yes!" Kurt says, a little bit too shrilly.

"You've been in there forever."

Kurt bites his lip, concentrating hard to keep it playful.

"Old people take longer. Have your donut."

Thin streams of blood run down his leg. He goes fast and rough, not caring if he misses a patch here or there. When he's done he pulls the basin's plug, scoops up clumps of hair from the drain and dumps it into the toilet. He takes out the face mask, skims the instructions and slathers it onto his face. He needs extra to plaster away his beard. When he's done he takes the shower cap, snaps it over his head and looks into the mirror.

*Pretty convincing.*

He runs through the plan:

Go into the apartment, get into the bedroom as quickly as possible and tell Kelly I have a headache and that she has to leave. Be firm. It's my home, not hers. As soon as she is gone, get Wolfgang. Then clean up everything, leave no trace. Get back to the apartment and start packing. Remember Wolfgang. Leave town. There are lots of other places where people would appreciate our skills. New York, for instance. Yes, New York.

He just needs to remember to get Wolfgang.

He takes a deep breath, twists the doorknob and steps into the lounge.

"Finally! You rea..."

A pause. Kelly blinks.

"Who the hell are you?"

"Hawooooooo!" Wolfgang howls. Kelly actually turns to look at him. In that moment, Kurt jumps forward. Kelly might be fat but she's not an old lady. She jumps up and over the back of the couch in an instant, putting the couch and the coffee table between her and the man wearing Gran'ma's dress with the face mask.

"Help!" she screams. She puts everything into it.

Kurt jumps the coffee table. There's lots of soap still on his legs, the foam turned pink with blood. The dress rips. He bounces onto the couch and the momentum knocks it over. The frame snaps. Kurt falls down hard, clicking his teeth together.

Kelly is at the door fumbling with the security chain. She slips it out, opens the door and shouts "Help!" before Kurt bashes the door shut and smacks her face into it. He has her by the hair, pulls her back, then slams her again and again. She goes limp and collapses, leaving him with a handful of hair and staring at the blood smeared on the door. He slips the security chain in place.

"That wasn't part of the plan, was it?" Wolfgang asks.

"Shut up, shut up, shut up."

"What are you going to do, Clever Carl?"

"I'm trying to think!"

"Boys who shout don't get pudding," Wolfgang says wisely.

Kurt ignores him. There's a teenage girl that he can add to his collection of persons in the bathtub.

He drags Kelly by the ankles. She leaves a snail-trail of blood from her mouth and nose. There's a narrow aluminum strip on the floor at the bathroom doorway. Her teeth catch on it as he drags her. He yanks harder. A tooth clips out and Kelly is screaming again. Kurt grabs her by the hair and drives her face into the ground. She goes quiet.

He dumps her on top of her grandmother. The bath is quite full now. He takes a second to rest. In the bathroom mirror he sees the face of a mad stranger; sweat has run furrows through the face mask and the shower cap has popped loose on the right hand side of his head, showing hair that is still stubbornly gelled into a teenager's spikes.

There's a knock on the door. It is hard and deliberate, like a cop on a TV show.

"Hallo? What's going on in there? I heard screaming."

It's John Butch. Kurt thinks about ignoring him but then Wolfgang whispers.

"He stays right below this apartment, remember? The couch, which I'm lying on—where you *forgot* me—fell over right above him. Do you remember?"

"Yes."

"He knows," says Wolfgang. "He. *Knows*."

There's only the bathroom window left. Kurt climbs on top of Kelly and her grandmother. Her soft belly shifts beneath his feet. She groans. He doesn't care. He pops out the window with his fist. Most of it goes. He grabs the one jagged tooth remaining and wiggles it out. He tosses it through the window.

The apartment door crashes open.

"What?" John says.

Then, "Kurt!"

"He saw me! He saw me!" Wolfgang yells, only the voice comes from the bathroom.

Kurt is glad Wolfgang isn't with him right this second. Wolfgang shouldn't see this. He deserves better.

Kurt is halfway through the window, his half-shaved legs sticking out stiffly behind him, the frame holding him by the stomach, when John opens the door.

"You sick bastard!"

Kurt looks down at the sheer drop. Three floors down. Nothing but concrete and an overflowing garbage can. There is a car parked across the road. The driver has rolled down his window and is looking up at Kurt sticking through the window like a pimple on the building's skin.

He can survive the drop but not if he goes head first. He feels John's hands around his ankles, the grip like a vise. In spite of everything, Kurt feels relief. He doesn't want to go to prison but he doesn't want to die either. They are mutually exclusive at this point.

"Pull me in!"

For a moment that's exactly what John does. Kurt feels the shards of glass mincing his gut. Then John stops. He starts pushing.

"What are you doing?"

"Shut up, Kurt."

"Noooooo!" Wolfgang howls.

Kurt flails his arms but can't find a grip on the building's face. He shrieks as the glass slices him. Then his belly shifts, it's like the window frame stretches wider. He is distinctly aware of the cold air on one side and the stuffiness of the bathroom on the other. He's so glad that Wolfgang is not in the bathroom to see it.

Then he's through. He hangs for a second, sees the man across the street spilling from his car, and then the pavement rushes towards him.

"Noooo!" Wolfgang howls and John looks back into the lounge with wide eyes.

It is the last thing Wolfgang says.

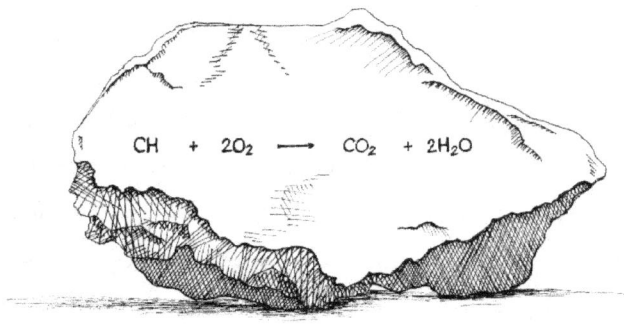

$$CH + 2O_2 \longrightarrow CO_2 + 2H_2O$$

## BLACK ROCK

by Liz Crossland

Black lace draws my gaze. It's the pattern of swirls and daisies, patches of skin visible in the holes of the embossed surface. The soft flesh that I want to stroke, but can't. The club rules are "No Touching". You have to sit with your hands under your legs. My fingers moisten against the faux leather seat. It's been a while.

This one isn't her. The hair's too short, undercut at the nape, filaments highlighted by the blue neon light. She stares at me through hazel eyes, narrowed as if to say *you're filth.* I want to scream at her, to tell her we aren't all like that. I'm on a rescue mission... and does she know my girl, my @Rapunzel? But there's a bouncer watching us, arms folded into his black suit.

I tuck a £20 note into the dancer's knickers, then limp to the bar across the beer-dribbled floor. Girls spin and twirl on stage to the music like the sirens of old, calling out to sailors for their adoration. I ignore them, sipping my pint. The lager's warm but refreshing. As the bubbles pop in my mouth, my shoulders lower and I look around.

Since the accident, I don't drink often. It interferes with my medication. But this club – *Rocks* – well, it's my last shot. If she's not here, I've lost her for good. And I'll go back to my twenty-year-old, twisted life. I raise my hand to my face, feeling the deep grooves and scars. You could trace our relationship in this crippled body: here is where she first pushed me against Black Rock, my back slamming into the stone. Here's where she gripped my arm, saying we had to get out of this town. And this is the scar she left on my heart, the night she disappeared.

Who else would want me, except @Rapunzel? Her last tweet, one year ago:

> **Rapunzel** @Rapunzel
> Find me

And my reply:

> **Steve** @hopelessromantic
> I'm coming, darling. You'll be safe with me.

\* \* \* \* \*

Our town: a small industrial city in northern England. It's like stepping back in time, with its Victorian streets and cracked pavements. But go to the surrounding suburbs, and a different world of eighties concrete and

American-style shopping malls dot the landscape. Our school was a modern comprehensive, built on the edge of town.

I was fifteen when I first met Rachael, in a Science lesson after lunch. She stood at the classroom door, bag hooked over one shoulder. I was transfixed. She had long hair and lace tights, pulled tight under her school skirt.

Mr. Porter looked up from his desk. "Those stockings are against the school uniform policy," he said, marking her name on the register.

Rachael shrugged and took a step into the room. She blinked as she looked round at us all; at the scattered textbooks and test tubes.

"Well, you're here now," said Mr. Porter. "Partner Steve: he'll get you started."

I half-raised my hand to show who I was, then pushed aside my piles of notes and exercise books to make room. Rachael stood for a moment before perching on the lab chair next to me, folding her hands on the desk.

"How come you don't have a partner already?"

I looked at her, taking in the eyelashes spidered in mascara, at the hole in her nose where a ring should be. I considered telling her about my perfectionism—OCD the doctors called it—about how every time I get a lab partner, they ruin my system of categorising samples and ingredients and file cards. But the way she was looking back at me: it was like she was sticking a probe into my brain. "I prefer to work alone," I said.

"Oh," she said. "A 'lone ranger'. That's fine by me."

She let me do all the work that lesson, yawning as she fiddled with something in her hands. My own hands shook more than usual while I measured chemicals and stirred solutions. When the bell rang, Rachael slid off her chair and ran out without being dismissed by Mr. Porter. He stopped me as I tried to leave the room.

"Keep her safe, Steve," he said.

"Yes, sir," I said. At the time, I assumed he was talking about dangerous chemicals.

\* \* \* \* \*

The next day, we had Science again. Rachael arrived slightly after everyone else. Her eyeliner was smudged, surrounding eyes bloodshot and swollen.

"Hey, 'lone wolf'," she said.

"What happened?" I said, pausing in my note-taking.

She just shook her head and played with her fingers. Again, I did all the work. It was only when Mr. Porter came to monitor our experiment that she looked up. "Hey, sir." She flashed him a smile and shook her dark hair.

"Good work, Rachael," said Mr. Porter, examining the test tube in front of us. The mixture inside was the right consistency and acidity he was after.

"Keep taking the credit for my stuff," I hissed at Rachael when he continued his rounds.

She laughed, placing her hand on my thigh. "I will. Don't worry."

\* \* \* \* \*

## It's a Grimm Life

I went to the library that day after school, too worked up to walk home or play football. I kept seeing her eyes sparkling in the light of the Bunsen burner. I kept hearing her laugh, and there was something else. When she'd touched my leg, she'd activated some part of me I'd managed to ignore until now. Buried in school books and science, I'd not paid much attention to girls. But this particular girl—this silent one with the long hair and dirty mascara—there was something different about her. Mr. Porter had told me to keep her safe. But safe from what? I itched my leg where she'd touched it. There was a mark on my school trousers, an indentation as if she'd drawn a nail or something hard against it. When I got home that night, I found a fine scratch on my leg. It was as if she had marked me, branded me for her own.

\* \* \* \* \*

"Mind out!" Rachael had nodded forwards on the desk, eyes half-closed. I pushed her away from the Bunsen burner. The smell of singed hair hit my nostrils. Rachael peeled her eyes open, her eyelids heavy with sleep.

"What happened?" she said.

"You nearly set yourself on fire."

Rachael's hand flew to her head. She dragged her fingers through her hair, checking it was all there. And that's when I saw it. The ring on her fourth finger. Whitby Jet, it was, the polished black stone glinting in the flame of the burner. I swallowed.

"You saved me," said Rachael.

Warmth rushed to my face.

"You're my hero," she continued, locking her eyes in mine. "I can't afford to lose my hair." She stroked it with her left hand, with that marked left hand, the ring on her finger.

I swallowed. The scratch on my leg throbbed, as if in memory. When the bell rang, she disappeared without saying goodbye.

\* \* \* \* \*

"Where do you go every day after school?" I kept my eyes on the test tube, shaking it slowly.

Rachael shrugged. "None of your business. I thought as a lone wolf, you'd understand." She traced a biro heart on the lab top. Despite her best efforts to conceal it, the black Whitby stone caught the artificial light of the classroom. It winked at me: a black heart willing me on.

"And what's that ring you keep hidden?" I continued, unable to stop myself.

Rachael dragged her eyes up to meet mine. For a moment, the resolve in them seemed to melt, but then hardened. She uncovered her hand. The stone sat there, proud and bold. Black and unforgiving.

"You're engaged?" I said.

"We're destined to be together," Rachael snapped. "Whatever my parents and the teachers say."

"What about the other day?" I said, heat rising to my face. "I saved your hair from getting burnt. You called me your hero."

"Oh, little boy," said Rachael, rubbing the stone under her finger. "*This* is what love looks like, you loner. I need my hair long and lush for the wedding. That's all I meant."

"But you're fifteen," I said, my lip trembling. "You've got your whole life to meet someone."

Rachael's eyes widened and she paused for a moment. "Like you, you mean?" Her voice softened.

"Maybe," I said. "Look, I don't know who your fiancé is, but I've seen how you come in here, knackered every day. Is he really worth it?"

Tears wobbled on the rims of her eyes. "He's eighteen. He knows what he's doing."

"Mr. Porter said I had to keep you safe."

The tears evaporated as quickly as they'd come. "Oh, and you know better?" she said. "Loser." She covered her left hand with her right and refused to speak to me for the rest of the lesson.

When the bell rang to mark the end of the school day, I blocked Rachael's path. The panic was in her eyes as she tried to sidestep me. "I can't be late for Tony."

"He has a name, then," I said, the words sticking in my throat.

"Out of the way, loser." She elbowed past, hitching her skirt as she ran off down the hall.

I ran after her, pushing my way through throngs of students and stumbling down corridors. Her black head bobbed along as she slipped like an eel towards and out an exit. Through the door, I saw her making her way to an older boy who was revving his Harley-Davidson near the bike sheds. He had a floppy fringe and black jeggings, silver rings on every finger. As Rachael moulded her body around him, fumes kicked out of the exhaust. She stuck her finger up behind her, she knew I was watching. All I could feel was a knot in my stomach as she rode away, away from me.

* * * * *

I trudged home along the bike path, kicking the autumn leaves under my feet. I thought of the way she'd glared at me when I'd found out her little secret. And then those other moments, when she watched me quietly measuring our ingredients or washing test tubes. It was times like those when it felt like we were one with each other, her on the lab chair, me taking notes. I'd seen the way her mouth curled when I made a joke. She must have felt safe with me. I kicked a conker so it skittered down the path. I'd blown it. She'd never trust me again.

* * * * *

Ours was a terraced house in the centre of town. Mum was at work. I flicked on the kettle to make myself a hot chocolate, then climbed the stairs to my room two at a time. The walls were covered in maps of the solar system and diagrams of cells and atoms. I could lose myself for hours in here, tracing the patterns of constellations or staring out of the skylight at the moon. Not tonight, though. Tonight I needed some more physical relief. Ever since Rachael had stroked my leg, I'd been following a girl I found on Twitter. Her user name was @Rapunzel. Her tweets were an escape from the *loner* knockbacks of Rachael. And, if you said something nice to her, she'd send you a private picture. Unlike Rachael, where, apart from her lace tights, her body was covered in school uniform, @Rapunzel's pictures sometimes had the hint of a bare leg or the side of her chest.

I turned on my laptop and sat back on the bed, legs trembling in anticipation. *Damn Rachael*, I thought. What did an eighteen-year-old biker have that I didn't? Apart from a bike. I clicked on Rapunzel's avatar: a sheet of black hair thrown forwards over black-rimmed eyes. I was ready for some fun. Expecting the usual flirty tweets, I was surprised to see her latest tweet, three minutes ago:

**Rapunzel** @Rapunzel

Shit day. God, I'm fat. Need handsome prince to help let down my hair #trapped

Another tweet appeared:

**Rapunzel** @Rapunzel
so trapped #trapped

The electric light of the computer screen cast a blue haze. Tentatively, I replied to her thread:

**Steve** @hopelessromantic
@Rapunzel can I help? #trapped

She answered:

**Rapunzel** @Rapunzel
@hopelessromantic could be dangerous

I stared at the screen for a moment before replying.

**Steve** @hopelessromantic
@Rapunzel I can be your prince

My tweet just hung there, unanswered. I stared at the darkening sky through the window above me. Had I gone too far?

Then the screen pinged again:

**Rapunzel** @Rapunzel
@hopelessromantic DM me if you want to know

We messaged each other until 3am. I ignored the piles of homework on my desk, the lure of the television downstairs. I ignored the thought of Rachael on that motorbike, legs wrapped around Tony.

Rapunzel sent me more pictures; always blurred, always with those black locks hiding her eyes. In one, the hair curled over her breasts, skimming them like silk. I shut my computer screen and breathed hard. I typed on my mobile phone:

*Let me help you, beautiful*

Rapunzel's final shot was even more distorted. It looked like a rock with chiseled edges. One that would cut you if you got too close. Her black hair flickered across my retina: an imprint. She had me then; I knew it. No escape. Rachael was forgotten. At least, for the moment. I fell asleep, phone in my hand.

\* \* \* \* \*

## It's a Grimm Life

It was Double Science the next day: usually my favourite because I'd get to sit next to Rachael. But she sat several rows in front of me, slumped over the desk. When Mr. Porter held up a glass jar containing a pickled embryo, she pretended to retch. My eyes drooped as I copied notes off the board.

My phone vibrated in my pocket:

*Meet me at Black Rock tonight 8pm*

I clattered my stool on the floor as I nearly dropped the phone. Rachael turned and glared at me. There were dark patches under her eyes, like carved-out crevices. Her lip was torn as if she'd forcibly removed a piercing.

"Loser," she mouthed.

Maybe I shouldn't have given Rapunzel my phone number, but how else does a hopeless romantic rescue a damsel in distress? Phrases she'd used yesterday danced in my brain: *we're getting married; don't love him; trapped; help me…*

This was the second girl I'd met who was in trouble. If not Rachael, I may be able to save her.

\* \* \* \* \*

When the school day ended, I hung around the library with the other geeks: my usual haunt now. They'd put me in charge of overdue library books. Rachael saw me and smiled, a deep, knowing smirk.

"Do my homework for me, loser," she said. Then she ran off, to meet *him*. I watched her skip away with a heavy heart.

118

The librarian finally kicked me out. I hoisted my rucksack onto my shoulders. In my pocket I had eight pounds fifty, the cash I'd managed to lift from the "Fines" box. Rapunzel said we needed as much as possible.

\* \* \* \* \*

Black Rock was a short bus ride away, the rock a jagged edge silhouetted against the sky. I sat down on a ledge and waited. In a heartbeat of impatient boredom, a hand covered my eyes before I could turn round. Her lips bit against mine. In the darkness, her features were all but invisible.

"But three weeks … he'll kill you," I said.

Her response was to pull my body closer to hers. As we pressed against the rock, I stroked her hair. After, she rubbed her hand across the front of my trousers. Blood heated my face. Light from my mobile phone glanced off a mascara-streaked eyelid.

"Did I hurt you?" I said.

"I need your help. To get away from him," she said.

"I brought the money," I said, handing over the stash.

She pushed it into her bag: a bag stuffed with tissues and make-up and condoms.

"Can I see your face?" I said, trying to brush the hair from her forehead. In the blackness, my fingers traced her cheekbones, the tiny nose. "You remind me of another..."

She cut me off, pressing her lips once more against mine.

"Forget her," she said. "It's safer this way."

## It's a Grimm Life

* * * * *

Next day, Rachael was late to Science, her skirt hiked up, displaying black lace. Mr. Porter sent her straight to isolation. As she passed my desk, I noticed the jet ring on her finger jammed on hard. There was a ridge and a rim of blood.

"Get a good look," she taunted. "While you have the chance."

* * * * *

I met Rapunzel every day at Black Rock. Sometimes we kissed, other times we lay on the cracked earth. Always in darkness and I always brought her money. To plan her escape. To plan our future. What do I remember? Silky soft hair, the rough skin of her hand on mine. The face that she hid with those raven locks. The tickle of her hair on my neck and chest.

"What are your dreams?" she once said, sleepily.

"To see the world. To travel," I said. "How about you?"

"I want to bring the world to me," she said. "Who needs travel?"

I folded my body round hers, cradling her from behind on the picnic blanket. My fingers traced the inclines of her hips and her soft stomach. It was only when I tried to clasp her hand in mine that she pushed me away. I covered her with my black school blazer and she lay still, exhausted.

* * * * *


The following week, Rachael turned up to Science with her long black hair shorn off, the remnants spiked up with hair gel. It was another lesson on embryos. This time she ran to the bathroom when Mr. Porter lifted up the jar. I stared at the perfectly-formed shape, jelly-like in its curled-up position. Sunlight cast through the windows, highlighting its tiny fingers and toes in red. Later, Rachael disappeared. Permanently excluded, they said. There were whispers of pregnancy. I took little notice: I was meeting Rapunzel later and she was going to leave him.


* * * * *


The bus climbed the hill in the direction of Black Rock. I rested my head against the window, watching the water droplets form and disperse. The glass was cold, it made my nose ache. As the bus lurched along, each rev of the engine sent a jolt through my stomach. I remembered our last meeting, the light of my mobile phone casting a harsh blue light on her stomach. She'd touched it from time to time, as if checking it was still there. I frowned at the gathering darkness outside the window. She was going to leave him. I repeated the words in my head to the rhythm of the wheels. She was going to get on the bus back to town with me. I'd finally get to see her face; those haunting dark eyes under the masses of long hair. I'd take her back home with me. Mum would understand when we explained. She was a fugitive. She'd be safe with me and my family.

121

## It's a Grimm Life

We'd lie on my bed under the stars, her face exposed to the moonlight. No more meetings here at Black Rock. No more secrecy or lies. Then, in the morning, we'd take the train to Cambridge. I had an interview with the university. We'd find a flat, ready to move in together in September.

The bus shuddered to a halt. "Your usual stop," said the driver. I stepped off the bus with my rucksack into the cold. Rain was lashing against my face. I pulled my blazer around me and staggered round the rock to our usual meeting place. Here there was some protection from the elements. Below me, the lights of the town twinkled in the darkness. In those terraced streets was our safe haven. I just needed her here, now, with me. Then we could hail the next bus and escape the rain.

I leant against Black Rock, waiting for her arrival. She was fifteen minutes late. She was always on time. I bit my lip, shoving my hands into my blazer pockets. Jiggling to keep warm, I saw the bus I'd planned for us to get swerve past me on the wet road. Water was running in rivulets down the hill, trickling into the drains. I checked my phone. The screen was blank. Perhaps she hadn't managed to get away this time. My stomach lurched. I'd be back tomorrow and the next day until she showed up, if needed.

Stepping out towards the road, I heard the engine roar before I saw the bike, no lights to mark its passage. With a quick step back, I flattened myself against the rock. My left leg snapped as the bike's wheel clipped me. Shards of stone lacerated my face as I spun to the ground. The motorbike careered down the road, sliding from side to side, with no intent of stopping. Blood ran down my face. There was the smell of copper, like one of those Science experiments I'd done with Rachael. And then the pain in my leg hit; a wrenching stab, as if the shin was being peeled from the bone. As the bike roared away, my vision was too obscured by blood and tears to notice anything about its make or model. At least, that's what I told them in court.

* * * * *

The operation to save my leg left me lame. The doctor said I was lucky. As I ran my fingers over the jagged ridges on my face, the only thing I cared about was that @Rapunzel had stopped tweeting. There were no texts, no phone calls.

* * * * *

Winter turned to spring, and then to summer. I missed most of the school year. It seemed the logical thing was to get a job in the local library. Free internet access, for a start. I could pretend I was cataloguing books all day.

"What about your science potential?" the e-mail from Mr. Porter said. "You were Oxbridge material."

His words meant nothing. I had to find her. She's the only girl who let me rescue her like that. My good leg still twinges with the memory.

* * * * *

## It's a Grimm Life

It was eight months before she was back online. She was working at a lap-dancing club. One tweet, "Find me". Just like that. As if nothing had happened. And then she disappeared again. My e-mails to her were 'undeliverable'; she ignored my texts and I couldn't trace the number. So I trawled every club in the area.

\* \* \* \* \*

*Rocks* is the last one. Its garish fluorescent lights seem too obvious, too cheap for her.

It's been two years. She's not here as I scan the room, my eyes blurred from alcohol. I down my drink, ready to leave, leaning on the bar. The bartender raises his eyebrows at me, then, there's a hand. A shield over my eyes. A flick of black hair. An echo of the past. I can smell her; a dank, earthy scent like the peat under that once-familiar rock. Wordlessly, she leads me to an "Exit" sign. Something hard digs into my palm. We emerge into neon streetlight.

"You found me," she says, holding out her finger as I stare into spider-rimmed eyes.

Removing the plaster, I see the jet black ring, polished and cut. It's welded into her skin, surrounded by a ridge of purple bruising.

"You can't be her," I say. "No, not Rapunzel."

"Let's get out of here," she says.

I shake my head, turning to go, but Rachael waves a creased, blurred photo under my nose. The same dark ringlets curl over peach-smooth cheeks, so small and frail.

"She shares your love for science," she says.

And there's another photo, this time on a mobile phone. A tiny fist mixing flour into water; it's smeared over her face. I trace the delicate features on the screen—the button nose and deep brown eyes. Then I touch my own face, wincing at the memory. Rachael's gaze follows my fingers, noting the scars and crevices.

"What happened at the rock?" I say, but we both know the answer.

"You lied in court to protect us. Thank you." Tears form on Rachael's mascara-lined eyelids. This time they spill down her cheeks. I brush her cheekbones and stroke her hair. The filaments are soft and fine—and full of hair grips. As I stroke, I catch the pins with my fingers and pull them out. They ping on a drain cover, bouncing off onto the cobbles. Rapunzel's purple raven hair flows down her back, to her waist, like a river leading to that night of the rain, and the bus... and the accident. She twists the hair round her fingers. The coils quiver as I caress them.

"Tony...?" I say.

Rapunzel shakes her long, dark hair. It flexes in the moonlight like a constrictor. "He can't hurt us now."

We gaze at the baby on the screen, the open-mouth laugh full of innocence.

Rapunzel raises her eyes to mine. "It's our turn to save you." She traces her ring finger across my face. Then she takes my hand and leads me away from the club, my face burning where she had run her finger across the deepest lesion.

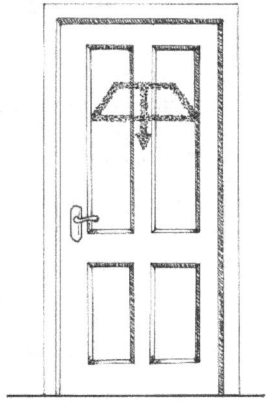

## THE WICKED STEPMOTHER

by Jessamy Corob Cook

Once, I wished for a daughter of my own, more than anything in the world. And my wish was granted. It was. It was.

Blanche is my stepdaughter, but I love her with all my heart. She dotes on her father; but I know I love her so much more than Lawrence ever could. He is rarely here these days, always away – business, if you believe it. But that doesn't matter to me. It's better this way. Just me and my lovely girl.

It was the night she turned sixteen. Not a little girl any more. (But my girl still. My girl, forever.)

I was just leaving the house, but I paused to look back one more time. It was late, but the summer twilight clung on, deliciously purple. I'm a wicked stepmother. I have done terrible things in my life, but...

But I love my girl.

The windows were bright, and flickering with moving figures. The pulse of Blanche's "just-a-few-friends" sixteenth birthday party throbbed down the front drive. I could feel it through the soles of my feet. I imagined it radiating down the road and bouncing like sparks off the leaves of the polite suburban hedges. I still felt out of place here; this wasn't my world. But Blanche was worth the sacrifice.

I had laid down the ground rules for the party: no drugs, no alcohol, no sex, the usual. And I very emphatically reminded her not to go into my study. Not under any circumstances.

She rolled her eyes. "Like I'd be interested. Anyway, it's always locked. So? Do you accept that I'm categorically mature enough to have a party unsupervised?"

And I had said "I'll give you till midnight, then I'll be back."

She didn't ask what I would be doing until then.

And so I said goodbye, as the guests began to pile in. I locked my study, and hid the key in the kitchen, on the third shelf up in the cupboard, inside the blue mug with the yellow stars on it. And now it was time to go.

I climbed into my car and headed out of town, towards the woods. It had been a few years since I'd come this way, but I knew it by heart. I pulled into the little car park, glanced at the glowing green numbers of the clock – 7:46 – and switched off the engine.

By day people come here to walk their dogs or go cycling or for picnics. I don't come here in the day. I sat for a few moments. I had made up my mind, but still I needed time. I have done terrible things in my life, but that night I did the most terrible thing of all. But I wouldn't think about that.

I locked the car and began to make my way through the trees, ignoring the footpath sign. The layers of rotting leaves muffled my footsteps, and the only other sound was distant birdsong. Deeper into the woods, the trees grew closer together and brambles snaked towards my ankles. It smelled of moss and earth and badger. The darker it grew the more at home I felt.

I plunged into the chaos of brambles, nettles and low-hanging branches, sometimes having to clamber, duck or crawl. My white trousers would be ruined – so this was why I always wore black in the old days! At last I pulled free of a vicious patch of thorns, and stepped into the clearing.

The pool was still there – clear and silver in the moonlight, with that strange violet blush, which you might have thought was a trick of the light, if you didn't know the colour of magic when you saw it.

And there he was, crouched on a rock at the water's edge, wet and slimy, staring into the pool. With his back bowed, and his long hair falling over his face towards the surface of the water, he looked like a weeping willow, and my heart almost – almost – stirred for him. But his greyish skin, and his ridged spine repulsed me. Ugly creatures get no sympathy, in the human world or in ours.

He did not look up as he spoke.

"So ... the time has come. The girl is sixteen."

He sounded strangely young, his voice smooth and slippery as the rock he crouched upon.

"Yes, she's sixteen," I replied steadily. "She's having a lovely birthday. She's having a party. With her friends."

"It is time," said the creature, "to keep your side of the bargain."

"Actually, no. You didn't keep yours."

"I did."

"I asked for a child of my own. Blanche is my stepdaughter – that could never be the same."

Oh, Blanche, forgive me. The lies were to protect you. I swear.

"You could never have a child of your own," he said. "Only mortals can have children. You know that. I gave you the closest thing you could have, and you were happy. Now the time has come. We had a bargain. Give her to me."

"No."

Slowly he looked up from the pool, and straight towards me. His big, yellowish eyes gazed at me.

"Give her to me by midnight tonight, or I will take her."

Before I could reply he had leapt from his rock and into the pool with a splash. I watched the ripples flick slivers of moonlight out across the water.

"You will never have my girl," I called after him.

I have done terrible things in my life, but sometimes that is the only way, when you love someone and just want to keep them close.

I turned and strode away through the trees, twigs and thorns clawing at my face. Once I stumbled, and though the shock of it spilled out the tears I had been holding back, I caught myself on a branch and kept walking, breaking into a half-run as the trees began to thin, till I came to the car. I got in and slammed the door behind me.

I have made bargains with creatures like him before. Their magic is earthier and colder than ours. A witch's magic is powerful, but it is a magic of fire, wild and uncertain; theirs is a magic of the wood; ancient, with no feeling and no mercy. For this reason there is a lot they can do that we can't, despite their primitive minds. They do not spend years studying their art as we do. They are creatures of instinct.

I have made bargains with many, and none have got the better of me yet.

But I have never before had so much to lose.

I started the car, and watched the lights flash on. The green numbers of the clock said 11:12. It might have happened already.

I have done terrible things in my life, but tonight I did the most terrible thing of all. I locked my study, and hid the key in the kitchen, on the third shelf up in the cupboard, inside the blue mug with the yellow stars on it.

And I made sure that Blanche was watching.

I might not be too late. If I left now, drove fast, I might still be able to stop her.

I didn't. I began to drive, slowly, the long way round. I pulled into our drive at exactly 11.57, and realised I had changed my mind – all I could think of was getting there before it was too late, and stopping her. I burst out of the car and ran. Up the drive, through the front door, leaving it flapping open, up the stairs, up to the forbidden room.

I was too late.

The door was gaping open, and Blanche's friends were clustered about, babbling. Some were frightened, some confused, some giggling – too drunk to know what was going on. I spoke loudly and clearly, making them all jump and squeal.

"Get out."

They turned and started jabbering at me, "Something's wrong with Blanche, we need an ambulance, we need to..."

"Get out," I said again, and though I didn't raise my voice they all fell silent. Blanche had told me that I give most of her friends the creeps. Well, with good reason.

I moved aside to let them pass, and they tramped downstairs without another word. I stepped into the study.

There she lay – my beautiful girl – perfect as ever. Her rose-petal lips were parted slightly, and her eyes were open. Her golden halo of hair looked so fine that had I not known better I'd have thought a breeze would stir it.

As the clock on my desk began to strike midnight I felt a bony hand on my shoulder.

I turned, catching the creature off his guard, so that I was able to fling him backwards, and send him smashing into the wall.

He scrambled to his feet. Blood, so dark it was almost purple, was trickling from the corner of his mouth.

"What have you done?" he gasped. "What have you done to your own daughter?"

"What I had to," I replied.

I bent down and stroked her lovely face. It was cold. Because my curse had turned her to stone the moment she opened my office door.

"Do you want her now?" I murmured though my tears. "Do you want my girl? Will you love her now?"

His eyes widened, and he shrank against the wall, breathing through his teeth.

"Will you love a lump of rock? Will you care for it day after day, night after night, for the rest of your pitiful existence?"

The creature gave a howl, bounded down the stairs, and was gone.

"I WILL!" I shouted after him.

Then softly, in Blanche's stone ear, stroking her stone forehead, "I will."

## CAST ME ADRIFT ON BIRDSONG AND ASH

by Carmen Tudor

She sat with her back to him and faced the window. He approached her, his dear Elsa, and stopped short. His outstretched hand, so close to fingering the roughness of her sleeve, dropped away. Once upon a time he would've touched her tenderly. Those were the days when they still shared smiles, and laughter, and love. Those were the days when she wanted to be here, with him. When she wanted this life and a little son, maybe.

"Elsa, I'm going out."

She didn't turn. At first Dessy watched her reflection in the window and noted how her eyes never left the lighthouse's tip in the distance. The steady rhythm of the pulsing light gleamed in her wide eyes. Then he cast a rueful glance to the fore, where the stone walls and softly smoking chimneys backed up right to the little cobbled courtyard outside the window. The Kent village was pretty in its way, but he knew she'd never see any of it.

"Go," Elsa replied. "You'll be back."

Dessy stepped away from his wife. "I'll come back as ever, I will."

Out on the shingle, his footsteps crunched and sank. He made his way toward the water as the sun rose over the eastern darkness. Each ebb and flow promised to cast him adrift, he thought. Cast me adrift. But, as Elsa had said, he'd be back.

After pulling a crumpled tarp off the boat, Dessy tugged it toward the water. He pushed the ten foot cedar and fir skiff along the water's edge until its square stern was all that remained on land. Giving one final push, he let the waves carry her forward. He waded until the cold waters rushed at his knees and, with an easy lope, jumped into the craft. His gaze steadied on the little, far off house. No fire and no warmth. The grate by his wife's feet held only ageless cinder. He turned his attention then to the empty half of the boat. Big enough for a large catch. Big enough for a small child.

As the sun rose above the tiny fishing village, Dessy cast his nets. The shrill cry of gulls overhead sang out in harmony with the sloshing of the waves and the click-tug of the grating oarlocks. A rhythm of sea and life, Dessy thought. Cast me away.

The hours passed evenly. The bottom of the skiff remained bare. Dessy hoped a single fish, something with marred scales, even, would feel his need and offer its life. He knew Elsa wouldn't be happy. It had been so long since they had tasted wine or cheese. Their parched lips waited daily for the fish Dessy promised. But daily they met an empty plate and Elsa, whose wan cheeks gave up their bloom long ago, would then cast her stones.

At day's end, Dessy pulled the skiff onto the shingle. Dragging its dead weight, he lingered only long enough to cover her up with the crumpled tarp. The wood smoke in the air hung lazily over the rooftops of the cottages, trapping the voices and scents of bee-liquor and ale emitted from the distant inn's shuttered windows.

*Row her down to Hero's Arms*
*Row her down and stay your feet*
*For here the poor-blood's mead is sweet*
*To give to him what he can never win.*

The old shanty was the same one his father had sung years before. When food was scarce and crying wives dried their tears on their children's names. Even Dessy's father had found happiness at the bottom of a tankard. But unlike his father, Dessy gritted his teeth against the temptation and kept walking.

Once inside his home, he closed the door and found his wife sitting by the window.

"What have you got?"

Dessy shook his head. "Not a thing."

Elsa's shoulders shook. She took a shuddering breath. "Even the dogs in the street eat more than me. What's to become of us?" She stood from her chair. Pulling her woolen shawl aside, she showed Dessy her protruding collar bone and upper ribs. The skin there was so taut he thought if she fell she might simply shatter to pieces. She was brittle that way. He said nothing. The meager swell of her belly remained covered, and that is where his look fell to.

"You go over tomorrow morning. I don't care what you do, but I won't die for your sake. Do you hear? I'll leave you afore that. Do you hear? You'll come and I won't be here no more."

Dessy nodded. Elsa resumed her chair in front of the blackened night-time scene. A lighted window twinkled and, in the distance, the lighthouse shone its warning.

\* \* \* \* \*

The skies were clear the next morning. Choppy breezes tipped the skiff about on the rollicking waves. It was on a similar day that Jed had been taken. His short keel, along with his wasted spirits, had sunk him like a stone. Just like that, he was gone. Dessy threw out his nets and waited.

Nothing below the waves stirred. Every so often a string of sea wrack got caught in the nets. On more than one occasion Dessy had pulled the nets up to find the green slime clinging on in place of a fish. He'd learned not to fall for the sea's tricks, but instead to wait for its truths. The morning time passed to afternoon. The swish and sway of the water cradled Dessy about until his heavy eyes closed. A gull squawked loudly and the man righted himself. Out in the quietude of the salty mists, it was so easy to get lost in dreams. It was so easy to remember a time before Elsa when, as children, Dessy and Jed combed the shingle for a treasure to find. It was so easy to get lost, to sink, he thought. Cast me down.

Dessy's net dragged toward the sandy shoal so that as the skiff rolled into shallow waters, he was soon awash along a sand bar. Struggling with the nets, he tugged them up, but something below the water, something of force, pulled back. The skiff rocked, and Dessy lowered himself back into the filling boat.

The sun shone clearly overhead. The sky was bright, but Dessy had no time to gaze out at a longed-for object. The things that mattered were the things he held within reach. The net, he reasoned, had no slack. The net was being pulled along. He pawed wildly at the thing to extract its lengths from the water. As he dragged the knotted net back into the skiff, he saw that no piece of seaweed was caught. There, glinting in the light of the sun, were scales. Dessy cried out as he watched a beautiful oval-shaped, almost diamond, flounder flip about.

"What are you doing up here near the shoal?" Dessy said breathlessly. "Did you see the sun a-shining so very bright, eh?"

The flounder's mouth opened and closed. Its slick body heaved and Dessy dried his tears.

"I must thankee for coming, though it be such a shame. But how is it to be helped?" He ran his finger along the line of sharp tubercles.

The fish, as it continued to flip and struggle, opened its mouth again. "Throw me back."

"Throw you back?" Dessy asked. "'Cause why? What would my Elsa say?" After a moment's hesitation, he added, "There'd be some yarping about that."

"Can't you see my place is here, in the water? This is where I belong. It's my place."

"But of course it is; you're a fish." Dessy laughed. He studied the flounder closely, as if making sure his eyes didn't deceive him.

"So go ahead and throw me back. Do hurry up about it, there's a chap." The fish gasped. "Men and fish are—" another gasp "—funny creatures. What one needs, the other wants. And what one wants will kill the other—" gasp "—and what kills the other is not what the one really needs."

"Needs? I think you speak riddles."

"Nay, nay. They're wants, to be sure."

Dessy picked up the flounder. Reaching out, he guided the fish into the water. "Eh? Well, all right then. Here you go. Careful now, and mind the nets."

The flounder wriggled its fins and swam away.

Dessy grabbed the oars. He steered the skiff back to shore.

Running over the crunching shingle, he passed the inn and the other little cottages, and pushed open his own front door. Elsa stood by the window. If she'd been looking she would have seen the mad dash through the village.

"Elsa, it's a miracle."

"What did you catch?"

"I caught a flounder bigger than any I ever saw."

Elsa spun around. "You done it. Here I was thinking you a Jonah of the worst type, with me nearly dead from want and you in ruin. Where is it? Let me have it."

Dessy clung to the door frame as he caught his breath. "I put him back."

"Let me have it."

"No, my wife. I says he be gone back."

Elsa's eyes narrowed. "What? I thought you said you put it back."

"Why, I did. I did put him back."

Elsa fell into her chair. Crystal tears rolled down her cheeks. Her bony knuckles gripped the frame of the chair.

"Don't cry. It was right; he asked me to. If you was there, you'd have done the same. It wants no looking at."

"If I was there, I'd have measured it good to quiet the squirming, I would. I'd have brought it home for supper, I would."

Dessy's hand fell away from the door frame. "Not this fish; it was enchanted-like. My Elsa, it was princely. Proper princely. I'll see you right yet."

"See me right?" Her eyes glowed like burning coals. "Says to my father he'll be a good husband. Says to my mother she'll never want. Pah. Poorhouse, more like."

Dessy removed his hat and mangled the floppy thing in his hands. "One more mouth to feed ain't much."

Just like that, the fire went out. "You expect to keep another mouth? No. You know my plans is good. Send him to work, then apprentice him at age."

Dessy's fingers stopped working the worn fabric of the hat. It slipped from his grasp and fell to the floor. "I never did like trade."

"You freed it?"

"Fancy I let him go, I did."

"You spared it 'cause it bade you do so?"

Dessy coughed; he stooped and picked up his hat. "Vero nihil verius, like I told y—"

"You got naught in return?" A new light shone in Elsa's eyes.

"Why should I have?"

"For all your book-learning, Dessy, all you know is rubbish and words. 'Cause you saved it."

Dessy peered at his wife. "I reckon as I did. But what on't?"

"You're going back over in the morning.  You're a-tell it you're in hopes of somethin' in return as you spared it the pan."

"I don't know about that."

"Your nets, Dessy.  Take your nets and tell it you deserve a reward for your deed.  You tell it so."

Dessy nodded.  "I can't say as I'll find him again, but I'll go much as ever.  And if he is about, I'll tell him what you said."

\* \* \* \* \*

Dessy rowed out to the shoal.  He sat in the skiff as a heavy cloud rolled over.  Before long the cloud opened and a large raindrop plashed down onto his cheek.  As he wiped the water away, a voice at his side startled him.

"It's you again," said the flounder.

"Me again."

The flatfish blinked its big, round eye.  "I say, where are your nets today?"

Dessy thought a moment.  "Today I'm not for fishing.  Today I'm for a-talking."

"Ah, ideas.  The way of kings.  The way of gods.  Talk then," said the flounder, "and I'll see if I can't match you wit for wit."

"My wife, see.  She says it ain't proper to spare you the pan and return of empty hands."

"Oh.  I thought it was something like that," said the flounder.  Ducking its head down into the water, it took a breath and then resurfaced.

"Go along if you must. We'll see if we can't do something about your wife."

Dessy reached out and patted the scales of the fish. "Thankee, I'm sure."

He bade goodbye to the flounder and left the darkening skies of the sea. The singing voices of the inn barely reached his ears as he passed by and made his way home.

As Dessy approached his front door, he looked down at the step. Someone had left a hot loaf of bread. The steam rose to his nose and carried the scent of rich, freshly baked crust. He picked up the loaf, entered, and met Elsa by the stove.

"Look what the fish sent ye. It's a miracle, my Elsa."

Elsa took the loaf from Dessy's hands. "Is this it? You spared it and this is it?" She threw the bread down onto the table. "Go back. In the morning I want you to go back. I don't care how you do it, but I want more. Tell it your wife won't stand for this."

Dessy sighed and nodded.

The flounder's words came to him in the night. They were words he wasn't sure he understood, but they were ideas he himself had felt in his breast.

Want.

Need.

Place.

The next morning the sun was hidden. Maybe it was tossed aside by an unkind father, he thought. No. An unkind wife. Cast me back.

The thunder rolled and Dessy's little skiff crashed about on the waves of the dark water. Unseen things lurked just below the surface, he thought. If the beautiful little flounder had come from somewhere below, what other secrets were hidden? Good things? Bad things? Where were the starving, pearl-eyed Jed's of the world? Tide-taken and anchored to the bottom of the sea with seaweed fetters?

The flounder poked its head above the water. "Hallo! There you are."

Dessy tilted his head to the side.

"You're not very happy," said the flounder. "What ails you, then?"

"Not such wery bad things. Only, I wonder sometimes whether want will kill us all. Want and need."

"What is it you want? What is it you need?"

Dessy grimaced. He pulled his coat tight around his throat and wiped the splashing seawater from his eyes. "Contrariwise, I don't want none on't. But I need it all. The lighthouse yonder. The whole sea. Give me the ocean." Dessy laughed. The skiff turned about on the ocean's roiling waves. One of the oars loosened from its oarlock and threatened to slip into the water. Dessy grabbed it before it disappeared. The little fish watched. "Give me all the ocean."

"I'm not sure I could do that, old boy," said the flounder.

"She commands it, she does."

"She wants it?"

"She needs it." Dessy sniffed. The rain fell heavily and the skiff soon resembled a small bathtub. The water rose and the skiff lowered.

"Give and take are two different things."

The man agreed.

"You see, if I give you what she wants, I'm giving up what you and I need." The flounder blinked its eye and flapped its fin at the surrounding water.

"I see."

"I thought so," said the flounder, and again opened his mouth to speak. A crashing crack of thunder drowned out its little voice. Dessy covered his ears. Waiting for Dessy to put his hands down, the flounder tried again. "I'll tell you what. You go home and you'll both have what you really need. How does that sound? No more, no less."

"She wants no more bread. But I thankee kindly."

"Well, then. No more bread. Only what you need, understand?"

Dessy gripped the oars. The stinging rain lashed at his face as the ocean rose and heaved. He looked from the waves to the flounder. "Why, that sounds mighty good of ye."

"I say, you'd better get along."

"I reckon as I will. I'll go right away." Pumping the oars with all of his strength, he watched the flounder while rowing ashore. The flatfish kept its one little eye on the fisher as he vanished into the mists of the storm.

Dessy struggled as he pulled the skiff up onto the shingle. His hair, his clothes, and his boat were full of water. Although each step was labored, he didn't stop until the crumpled tarp was safely over the skiff. The chimneys of the seaside village puffed out the characteristic wood smoke. Dessy's shivering form lumbered through the streets as he made his way to the cold cottage. A single, lost gull flew over the rooftops and settled above his door. It flapped its wings and, Dessy thought, blinked at him.

Dessy threw his dripping coat down and called to his wife. She wouldn't like the mess, but she didn't know what news he was bringing.

Elsa wasn't in her chair by the window. The light of the lighthouse was already coursing over the seas. The windows of the cottages twinkled their firelight. But Elsa wasn't sitting and watching. Dessy looked to the stove. Yesterday's half-eaten loaf of bread remained on a board, but Elsa wasn't there waiting. Dessy turned around and searched the four corners of the cottage. When he was sure she wasn't inside, he ran back out into the street. His heart, although heavy, was eager to tell his wife of what the flounder had said. His lips opened and closed as the fish's mouth had done when he'd pulled it out of the water the first time.

Dessy ran to the inn. Pipe smoke greeted the soaking wet man as he pushed through the door. Everyone shook their heads when he asked after his wife. They continued to drink and to sing and to smoke their glowing pipes.

Dessy ignored the pouring rain and ran through the lanes and down to the shingle. He crunched along the tiny stones until at last his boots reached the water's lapping edge.

"Little fish," he called. "Little flounder."

After a moment the flounder popped its head out of the water. Dessy couldn't hear its words over the tumultuous storm. He stepped forward until he stood ankle-deep in the water.

"I gave you what you both needed."

"Upon my life, what have you done? Where's my wife?"

"Only what needed doing. She's not harmed. Go home and look out your window."

"That's Elsa's window," Dessy replied. "Elsa's lighthouse. She lingered on't always—wanted it as her very own."

The flounder nodded. "So she did. And now, it's hers for all time if she chooses."

"Eh?"

"I say, it's hers for all time. The lighthouse. That is, hers until she no longer needs it."

## It's a Grimm Life

Dessy stumbled back over the shingle. He was cast along by thoughts of Elsa and the little flounder. By thoughts of bread and cinder. He took off his boots at his front door and, approaching the window, thought, Here I am, but where is she?

The lighthouse in the distance caught his attention. As the flounder had told him to do, he glanced through the glass and watched as the light pulsed its steady beam. Dessy's eyes widened and he took a step closer to the window. There, in the lantern room, a figure paced back and forth. Too far to see the image in reality, Dessy squinted and imagined that the shadowy form halted. In his mind the silhouette turned and looked out toward him.

\* \* \* \* \*

Time passed slowly and quickly in turns, as a long forgotten shipwreck might: anchored down, unseen, for an eternity and then raised to the surface to face the newness and beauty of sunlight. Each evening, once the balance was restored, Dessy sat in the chair by the window. Each evening he stoked the blazing fire in the grate and ate his supper. His little boy sat by his side, and his wife—no longer given to strange fancies of a lighthouse's unspoken promises—added a new piece of coal to the fire.

Buoyed with new hope, Dessy had taken on work, and worked hard. His own perseverance saw to his success, but he liked to think a helping hand, a funny little jewel of sorts, like something found winking in the silt, might have had something to do with the way things had transpired. Each evening Dessy lifted a toast to the strange flounder that had heralded his fortune, and said, "I've got what I need, I do. I always did, funny. But now I know it; for yesterday is gone, and tomorrow has not yet come." He would stop a moment and cast his wishes across the village and over the rocks. And each evening he held his tumbler a moment in front of the window as the lighthouse's steady beam caught the angle of the glass.

WHERE THE DAMNED GO

by Richard Tasonmart

*Sometimes, when I was mopping up sick, or looking at the paltry amount on my payslip at the end of each month, or on edge expecting another one of Merrick's practical jokes, I'd fantasise about having the place all to myself, sure. But that's all it was: a fantasy. And if I still went to confession, I'd ask Father Michael for forgiveness for that stupid wish, I would.*

*But I can't tell you where they went.*

*I can tell you the rest ... though, it won't help you find them.*

\* \* \* \* \*

I thought Merrick was playing one of his tricks when he said he'd seen a rat in the cellar. He was always pissing about like that: keeping the caretaker on his toes, pranking the deafie. When I went down, I was anticipating the punchline of his joke announcing itself at any moment. Nothing happened, and when I flicked on the cellar light, there they were. Rats. Three of them—staring at me from a shelf on the opposite wall.

I stumbled about trying to find something to bash them with. They watched me, furry heads moving back and forth in synch like puppets. When I attacked them with a broom, they leapt away before I could do any damage.

I spent a while looking for them among the discarded beds and dusty crates of old toys. All I found was a square of paper on the shelf where the rats had been, chew marks on the edges. An invoice from the previous pest control company. The box marked 'status' read *Unpaid*.

\* \* \* \* \*

The next day, one of the kids was feeding the squirrels in the orchard. Something scurried over and leapt to take the bread from her hand. It wasn't until the animal was in mid-air that she noticed the pointy head and the grey-black fur.

She screamed the place down, apparently—not that I heard it.

\* \* \* \* \*

"Eric, Mum wants to see you in her office," Merrick said.

I tried to ignore the smug little curve of his mouth as I read his lips, and went upstairs expecting another trick. I found Mrs. Merrick pacing back and forth with her eyes down on some papers in her hand.

"Jeremy says you want to see me about something," I said. I never call him Merrick to her.

"The rats," I saw her say. "The bloody rats are back. Have you seen them?"

I nodded.

"Look, I need you to sort it," she said. "We've the inspection next week and I just can't have non-children shaped creatures running around the home. You with me?"

"How would you like me to do it?"

"What do I care how it's done? I just want rid of them before they start pissing in the kitchen and give all the children Weil's disease. But do it properly. The last idiot clearly had no idea what he was doing."

I tried to suppress a smile.

"He didn't work out?" I said.

"We should have used you in the first place, Eric. Bloody Jeremy and his door-to-door salesmen. We never saw him do a jot of work.—"
She turned her back to me and I could no longer tell what she was saying.

"I'll need some things," I said.

She turned again to face me. "Get them then. And if you get rid of them for good, I'll make sure your Christmas pay packet has a little something extra, too."

Before I left for the shops, I had another look in the basement. From the shelf, six pairs of beady eyes looked back at me.

* * * * *

When we were kids, my sister was scared of rats.  Our family lived on the coast not far from where a huge cement pipe dumped all of the town's sewage into the sea—so we saw plenty of them.  I was more scared of the pipe, a huge drooling mouth that overlooked the bay, just waiting for a lost child to come by so it could suck them in.  Before my accident, I used to hear the wind blowing through it, a mournful horn.  Later, I would sometimes feel the sound, a vibration on my ears and on the nape of my neck.

I never understood the fuss about rats, though.  "They're just big mice," I would say.  But my sister would shake her head.

"Father Michael says when the end comes the rats will be left on earth to eat what God leaves behind.  He says you'll always find rats where the damned go."

* * * * *

When I returned to the cellar with the traps, eight rats sat on the top shelf to watch me lay them.

"Good news, boys," I said.  "I'm sending you home."

But the next day, the traps were empty and twelve rats were present to watch my disappointment.

Word spreads fast in the rat community and another day on, fifteen rats spread across two shelves, all turned up to see the incompetent

149

caretaker fail to get his Christmas bonus. I tried attacking with the broom, thinking I had a better chance this time given their greater numbers. But again, they were too quick.

I *had* managed to catch something this time, though. In a trap near the corner of the room lay something brown and furry.

*Bloody Merrick.*

I knelt down and retrieved the head and body of a decapitated teddy bear.

* * * * *

Soon they were everywhere.

Lucy, a sweet fourteen-year-old, orphaned by a plane crash, was in the shower. She reached blindly through the door for a towel and put her hand on something warm and wiry. Instinctively she opened her eyes and saw one of the little bastards lying on the towel rail. Another night, Margaret, a carer employed here, had been putting some of the younger children to bed when she pulled on what she thought was the cord to shut the curtains. A rat, nestled up on high, gave an agitated screech as she yanked its tail. This made Margaret tumble over backward which in turn made the children burst into laughter. That was until they saw what had made her fall, at which point they all ran down the stairs crying.

The strangest thing happened in the kitchen when Antonio was preparing the Sunday roast. He set down the chicken on the counter and went to fetch the marinade. Only, when he came back, the bird was missing. He told me he looked for it everywhere and was about to confront Merrick, assuming a prank, when he found the thing on the floor wedged in a hole in the skirting board.

\* \* \* \* \*

I imagined Merrick would approve of the sort of tricks the rats were playing, but the kid was growing increasingly distant, as if the rats had stolen his thunder. In an attempt to accelerate the clean-up in time for the inspection, Merrick was appointed my right-hand man by his Mum. Despite the extra help, I still caught nothing.

Late one night Merrick told me he could hear them behind the walls in the kitchen. We sat by the hole in the skirting board; me with a broom, Merrick with a hammer. After about ten minutes he started laughing his arse off, rolling around the floor. Thinking he had stitched me up I threw the broom at him. "You dick. There are no rats are there?" I stood up to leave but he was on me before I knew it, his arms clutching my shoulders, his face right up close to mine. His eyes were wide, his pupils like an oil slick over his iris.

"There are rats, Eric. I hear them all the time. In the walls, in the ceiling. In the fucking toilet bowl when I'm sitting on it." It was hard to read his lips they were moving so fast.

"Are you on drugs?" I asked, already knowing the answer.

"Fuck yeah," he said. "And I suggest you take some too. Because there is worse coming than rats. You're not supposed to cross him. But we did, Eric. And there's much worse than rats where he's from."

It was hard to tell, but I think he was giggling as he ran off. Later I found him asleep under the desk in the reception. I left him a glass of water and decided I deserved an early night so went back to my flat at the back of the orphanage.

* * * * *

The inspection went without a problem.

The rats were nowhere to be seen. Mrs. Merrick had told me that if they stayed away, my bonus was assured.

That night Mrs. Merrick bought some champagne, and when the children were in bed, we drank too much.

* * * * *

I woke up because the hairs on my ears and neck were being tickled by some unheard sound. It brought to mind the old sewer pipe. Unable to get back to sleep, I got out of bed and went to the window to let in some air. When I looked out I saw the light in Mrs. Merrick's office was on in the main building. The clock said it was three in the morning, which was far too late for her to be on site. I got dressed, grabbed a hammer from my tool box and headed over.

Once inside I went up to the first floor. On the way to Mrs. Merrick's office, I noticed a dormitory door was slightly open so I peered through the crack and saw a made-up bed in which no one slept. Out of curiosity, I stepped inside and saw that all six beds were made up and empty. I turned on the light and took a step back. On each bed was a rat. At once they jumped down and came straight at me. Three went past my left leg and three went past my right, as if I wasn't there. I turned and saw them darting down the stairs, followed by seemingly hundreds of other rats that had come from different rooms.

I ran to the dormitory opposite, and then to the next two along the corridor. All of them were empty. I banged on the carer's office. It was due to be Margaret that evening, but I went inside and found only a half-drunk cup of tea sitting on the desk, still warm to the touch.

It had to be a trick. One of Merrick's. One to beat the rats with. That was all I could think.

But I knew this was something else.

The thrumming in the air was stronger now, so strong I wanted to scratch my ears and neck. I went to the last door on the corridor and knocked.

"Mrs. Merrick?"

I pushed open the door to another empty room. The light I had seen from outside was coming from a lamp in the corner. I went over and switched it off. When I did, the room was still partially lit. The computer was on.

I went to her desk intending to shut down the computer, but instead my eyes were drawn to the window overlooking the orchard.

My breath caught.

Standing on the lawn in front of the tree line, lit by the security light and flanked on either side by hundreds of rats, were all the children. Mrs. Merrick and Jeremy Merrick were among them, as was Margaret and Antonio.

The only person I didn't recognise was the slim man standing at the front.

All eyes were on him. Even the rats.

He had something in his hands pressed close to his sharp face. As I watched him sway from side to side, I realised he was playing an instrument. He was playing a pipe.

The man noticed me and stopped playing. Immediately the thrumming in the air ceased. His congregation all turned at once to look at me. The man smiled, revealing a set of teeth as long and angular as his face. He gestured for me to come and join him, then said something that the congregation then all repeated. I read their lips: "Come."

Shaking my head I turned away from the window.

It had to be a trick. It had to be.

Trying to find another focus, I caught sight of the computer screen. There was a box asking: "DID YOUR DOCUMENT PRINT?"

I went to the printer and in the tray sat a single sheet of paper. An invoice.

As I read it my ears began to tingle again. Unable to stop myself, I looked out the window. The man with the pipe was no longer there, but I could see the last of his congregation, a collection of people and rats, heading into the darkened orchard.

The invoice was for a company called *Rattenfänger Solutions*. The amount requested for services rendered seemed reasonable to my eyes. At the bottom of the page was a box labelled 'status' with the word *Unpaid* crossed out in it. Next to that, someone had written *Paid in full*.

THE DEVIL'S CRAPPY JACKET

By Brett Parker

The Soldier met The Devil at a crossroads, the irony of which did nothing to abate his amusement. If he listened hard enough, he was sure he would hear an old Robert Johnson tune playing in the background; it would sound like an old record, scratchy yet somehow pure.

And he knew that when The Devil spoke, his voice would be smooth and deep, like the world's oldest blues man speaking into a microphone at some smoky, ill-lit bar. He could hear glasses clinking in the background, the sound of a hard, wooden match being flicked across a phosphorus striker, closely followed by a deeply indrawn breath, pulling in on a cigarette, then being expelled with a sigh, a soft, full sound, which hid behind it a wry and knowing grin.

## It's a Grimm Life

The Soldier felt a pang of emptiness when he stepped back on American soil. He had seen the videos on YouTube of other soldiers coming back from deployment, wives and children and friends rushing into their arms. He had none of these, so his homecoming was bittersweet and lonely.

While deployed in Afghanistan, his mother had passed away, following his father's passing three years prior. He was told it was a heart attack by his brothers over Skype, two weeks after her burial.

"We're sorry. I know you must be having it rough over there. We didn't want to burden you with all this...."

His brother's voice faded out as the realization sunk in. The Soldier stared through them, to the once familiar living room, the wall decorated in old photos behind them. He swallowed hard, to keep his composure, something he had been struggling to do these past months, when all he wanted to do was break.

Being a soldier in training was nothing like being a soldier trying to hunt down terrorists in a hostile city. There were no school-aged boys running around corners with IEDs strapped to their chests, thumbs over unforgiving triggers. These images forever haunted his faltering mind. The worst, seeing Sergeant Trippy's head exploding, a blossoming red spray that filled the interior of the Humvee. His nights were filled with this and the dreadful promise of what could be around the next corner.

But first was the coming home to nothing and no one. He knew that, someday, he would cry for his mother, and stop crying for the horrors within his war-riddled brain.

\* \* \* \* \*

Coming home, leaving Afghanistan and the service far behind, did nothing to quell his nightmares. He tried civilian life but it didn't take. He lost two jobs, ran out of money, and was evicted from his crappy little apartment.

"But Dave, I've got nowhere else to go!"

The static on the pay phone's line was making The Soldier's head hurt. The fumes from the truck stop, and the steady rumble of the diesel engines behind him, compounded the problem. And the beer he'd had for dinner the night before left a bitter taste in his mouth.

"I live in a single dorm room, bro. They don't allow it. Call Mark."

"I did," he answered, closing his eyes and trying hard not to hit something. "Mark says he and the family are in the process of moving, and don't have a place for me."

"Well, we kept some of the money from the sale of mom's house aside for you. Mark's got it. I spent mine on a car. It's a Corvette."

"I know, that's the fourth time you've told me."

"It's a nice car, man."

"Can I sleep in it?"

"What?" There was a pause on the other end of the line, and he could hear people laughing in the background. Is that what college was now? A constant party of over-privileged pricks, getting drunk and screwing their brains out while half a world away children blew themselves up and grown men got their brains shot out by faceless snipers?

"Nothing," The Soldier said. "Forget it."

"You know, I tell all my friends up here about my big bro the soldier ... " Dave was saying, but The Soldier was already hanging up the phone, looking about him to see if he could find the next ride out of the truck stop.

He now had absolutely nowhere to go, and no way to get there, and a debit card in his pocket that already felt as hopeless as his lot.

\* \* \* \* \*

The truck driver dropped The Soldier off at a crossroads, saying that was as far as he could take him--his stop was the refinery up the road.

"Company got eyes all ova' the place," he said, his eyes darting to the side mirror. "Ain't supposed to be givin' rides."

They were somewhere in Alabama. The Soldier forgot to ask exactly where before the trucker started pulling away, as if there was something behind him he was trying to flee.

"That would be me," The Soldier grumbled as he watched the taillights of the rig disappear in the haze of the setting sun. He looked down at the olive green duffle bag at his feet, then turned in a circle, eyeing the empty roads and flat, featureless land about him. Never in his young life had he felt such desolation and loneliness as he did now. He saw little difference in the twilit sky above him and the expanse of deserted fields about him.

It reminded him of the desert, and Sergeant Trippy, and the exploding kid.

"Maybe it should have been me," he said aloud. "At least Trippy had a wife and kids."

"You could always go back," said a voice behind him.

The Soldier spun around and nearly yelped at the sight before him. In the dead center of the crossroads stood a stooped man in a green coat and top hat. He was leaning on a shiny green cane, which somehow matched the sparkles in his light-green shoes. The only thing the misshapen man was wearing that wasn't green were his pants; they appeared plaid, but The Soldier wondered if he might find green threaded into them if he looked more closely.

"And you would be right," the strange little man said.

The Soldier shook his head. He'd been counseled and warned about PTSD, but hallucinating leprechauns?

The old man laughed. "I assure you, I'm no hallucination. And I most certainly am no leprechaun. They are smaller." He held up his right hand, holding the thumb and pointer finger about two inches apart. "And hairy. Very unkempt, my good man."

The old man removed his top hat, spread his arms wide, and bowed lower than The Soldier imagined possible. "I, my dear sir, am The Devil."

The Soldier stared at him.

Then looked down. Then looked around. Then he started to laugh.

The old man waved a hand at him. "I know, The Devil shows up at a crossroads in the middle of Nowhere, Alabama—how stereotypical. But I've got enough bluesmen to keep me company for a while. I'm in the mood for something a bit more … shall we say … challenging."

"I have a deal for you, young sir, which I believe may relieve you of your current distress and disappointment."

His laughter ebbed into a smirk. "What is it you think you have that I could possibly want?" The Soldier asked. "Your cane and your hat?"

"Goodness, no! I offer you pockets that are never empty, to steal away your poverty, to free you of worry, and make you whole once again. The answer to your prayers."

The Soldier smiled. "You, answering prayers," he replied.

"Sure, I am an angel after all," his lips parted in a toothy grin. "Then is there something you are afraid of? Surely it's a fear of something or other that is dragging your poor"—and he pronounced the next word carefully, almost delicately, and with no little amount of pleasure— "soul…down. I could alleviate all your fears."

"I am a soldier. I have faced down more horrors than any normal man should have to."

The Devil gave a wry grin. "Then prove it. Look behind you and behold."

The Soldier heard behind him a noise of a fingernail digging at plastic. He knew that sound, knew it well from his dreams. He turned his head, but not his full body. He did not trust the little person before him, man or devil. What he saw almost gave him a start, but he'd seen this before, knew the outcome, and suddenly believed quite irrevocably that the old man was the Devil. Nothing else could get inside his head besides something of a supernatural origin.

He turned his head back around and glared at The Devil. "Seriously? I already shot the boy once. I'm not scared of him coming back."

"Point taken. Then, if you aren't scared, put on my jacket."

The Devil offered up his green jacket, holding it out as if he were handing The Soldier an apple. He sighed, and took the coat, which felt like wool and something slithery. When he'd shrugged himself into it, the old creature pointed at the pockets. The Soldier rolled his eyes, and jammed his hands in. He pulled them out slowly, marveling at the rolls of bills of varying denominations. The Soldier carefully placed the money back into the pockets and shook his head.

"Maybe all those years of having to listen to screaming souls made you hard of hearing; I don't need your money, bub. You can have your jacket back."

"Think on it," the stooped, old man-devil said. "Think of the"— and upon the next word, his nose crinkled as if he smelled something foul, and his mouth spat out the word as if it were a rancid taste—"good … you could do. What else will you have of yourself?"

"I get a check from the Army every month and some savings. Take back your coat, it's starting to creep me out."

Suddenly, and although the old thing was standing a few body lengths away, he leaned in close, and seemed to cover half that distance without moving a single foot—a foot which now looked mysteriously like a hoof.

The Devil halted his removal of the jacket with a smile and upraised hands. "Okay, forget the money. Check the pockets again." The Soldier gave him a distrustful look. "Go on, you're safe. We haven't struck a bargain yet, so I can't touch you."

He hesitated a moment longer, then The Soldier reached into the pockets again. This time, he pulled out handfuls of quarters.

"For the slot machines in Vegas," The Devil said, smiling. "In Vegas, it isn't about the money, it's about the risk of losing. Surely that is something that haunts you."

The Soldier shook his head. "No, never was much of a gambler," he said, dumping the change everywhere.

The Devil looked frustrated. "Okay, check now."

He rolled his eyes again, yet did as asked. In his hands now were what looked like purple tokens, each imprinted with what could only be breasts.

"An unending supply of Tug-It Tokens from Pete's Porn Palace on 5th Street in New York City?"

This time The Soldier laughed.

"Check again—should be bullets."

The pockets were indeed filled with ammunition now. The Soldier smirked. "Could have used these six months ago, Beelzebubba. You're a bit late on that one."

"How about now?"

The Soldier was now holding a bottle of pills. Printed on the label, as if it were from a legitimate pharmacy, were the words *Spanish Fly*. He looked up at The Devil with a bored expression. "Okay, look again," he said.

The words had changed to *Love Potion No. 15*. "What's the difference?" The Soldier asked, and then doubled up with laughter.

The Devil waited patiently for him to finish. The Soldier wiped away the last of his tears. He had not laughed like that in some time—not since the time his brother Dave's ass hairs had all caught on fire from a wonderful mishap where he'd tried to light his farts afire. It was The Devil's turn to look at him wryly.

"Please?" he said, indicating the pockets again.

"Okay, but this is the last time. I really do need to start looking for a ride soon."

"Oh, I think this one will, shall we say, seal the deal." The Devil looked rather pleased with himself.

The Soldier reached into his pocket, and what he pulled out was old, tarnished, and heavy. It was a key, and from the looks of it....

"A skeleton key. Actually, THE skeleton key. That key will open any lock in existence."

The Soldier looked impressed. "Any door?"

"Anything with a lock on it: safe, window, door, car, box, whatever. It will open them all."

"And I can use it as many times as I want?"

"Anytime, anywhere."

The Soldier thought about it for all of five seconds. "What's the deal?" he asked.

The Devil smiled. "You have to wear the jacket—that's the deal."

The Soldier raised an eyebrow at him.

"It was a gift from the wife, it's not like I can't use it for something. And I'm tired of wearing the damn thing. So yes, you have to wear it. If you take it off for anything other than a shower, you lose."

"For how long?"

The Devil tapped an old, yellowed, broken fingernail against his wrinkled chin. "Seven years ought to do it."

"Not an Icee's chance in Hell am I wearing this frigging thing any longer than seven minutes." The Soldier began to remove the coat, and a panicked look stole across The Devil's face.

"No, no, you mustn't," he said, waving his hands at The Soldier. "If you take it off, she'll know I'm not wearing it!"

"Seven days."

The Devil's mouth fell open in shock. "That's no bargain! I could find a hobo to wear that forsaken thing for seven decades for an endless supply of booze if I wanted to!"

"Then why don't you?" The Soldier replied, then tapped his own finger against his chin in mockery. "That's right, what was it you said? I think your exact words were that you were looking for something more challenging, right?"

"But a week isn't long enough! What kind of bargain is a week's time?"

"I don't think it's really about you getting my soul now, is it?" It was The Soldier's turn to lean in close, although he had to take a few steps forward to do so. "It's about you being rid of this jacket for as long as possible. What you've already told me is that your wife knows if it is being worn or not, just not by whom. And you've had this thing on for how long now?"

The Devil looked down at his feet. "Four hundred thirty-seven years, eighty-three days, eleven-and-a-half hours."

"That's a long-ass time," The Soldier said.

"It itches me," The Devil said, looking up in the other's eyes. "Itches like mad."

"So even just a week would be a welcome break, wouldn't it?"

The Devil shook his head. "You forget—I am immortal. A week is like half of a half of a second to you ... or something like that. For me, it would be over just as fast as it had begun."

The Soldier thought on this for a moment. "Okay, I'll give you seven weeks. No more, no less."

\* \* \* \* \*

The sun was beginning to set on the quiet crossroads. The Soldier had been waiting four hours, seven weeks after the bargain was made, and The Devil was late. He decided his best option was to just take the damned jacket off and leave it in the middle of the road. He had one arm out of it when there was a slight clapping sound before him, and The Devil appeared in the road.

"Not yet!" he cried, waving frantically. "Leave it on!"

The Soldier glared at him, then slipped his arm back into the sleeve. Only then did The Devil stop his waving and jumping around. "Oh, thank goodness. Thank you, sir, thank you."

"Never thought I'd ever hear The Devil thanking me for anything," he replied.

The little demon smiled. "Oh, the last few weeks have been such a welcome respite. I wish I didn't have to take it back."

"Why don't you just accidentally lose it?"

The Devil gaped at him, as if The Soldier had just called him a derogatory name.

"That would be a lie. She'd know right away."

The Soldier rolled his eyes. "Then why don't you just tell her you don't like it?"

Again, the gaping mouth and wide, shocked eyes. "Why would I do that? Are you trying to get me killed?"

The Soldier laughed. "Is she really that bad?"

"You've no idea. She's a mean, mean woman."

"Don't they have some type of Divorce Court down there?"

"Then she and her mother would kill me. No, sir, I will have to take the jacket back. Only … I wonder if another deal might be possible."

"Here it comes," The Soldier muttered.

"No, it's not like that. I don't want you to keep it now, because I have to go home, and she'll be expecting to see it on me. What I would like is if you could meet me back here every seven years, and take it for another seven weeks."

"I think you need to find someone else," he said. "This thing does itch like crazy."

"But I could look out for you during that time! You would have a guardian ang… well, a guardian devil."

"Do you have any idea how much that would hurt my chances of getting into Heaven? Me ... helping you?"

And all of a sudden, The Devil's expression turned sly. His right eyebrow rose slightly, his eyes narrowed, and the left corner of his mouth rose in a crimped grin. "Ah," he said, "but you've already done just that, haven't you? You aided The Devil. There's a certain penalty for that. So, eventually, your soul is mine."

"You must have me confused with someone else."

The Devil shrugged his shoulders, "What did you do these past weeks?"

"Well, the first week I stayed in a five star hotel, eating and drinking everything off the room service menu while staying in bed watching endless hours of TV."

"Interesting. And what of the second week?"

Clearing his throat and mumbling under his breath, "I used the key to empty out some snobbish company's vault. Look, that was..."

The Devil dismissed any further explanation, "And following that?"

A smile and blush crept onto The Soldier's face, "Vegas. I had a little fun with some girls I met. The point of this was to forget, to push away..."

The Devil's hand came up, "And the fourth week?"

The Soldier squared off his shoulders, "A cosmetics lab had an unfortunate fire and the animals somehow safely escaped."

"The fifth?"

"I went back home. I visited some of my old haunts and visited my mother's grave. May have also broke into my brother's Corvette late at night to change all of the radio presets to country music and Spanish talk stations a few times."

"He is a particular sot, isn't he? And, what happened after?"

Following a long intake of breath, "I took my time traveling the countryside and stopped at all the tourist traps and restaurants along the way back here, where I could finally rid myself of this infernal garment."

"And here we stand, you, looking so proud of your achievements." The Devil chuckled ominously, and rubbed his hands together. A waft of brimstone carried upon the air, and The Soldier briefly imagined he could hear flames crackling in the distance. "Your seven week journey was filled with The Devil's intentions. You were found wanting in heavenly pursuits—slothful negligence, re-enervating the desire to accumulate wealth in the greedy, surrounded in lustful thoughts, igniting raging fires, envious of another's happiness and ignorance, and an extended gluttonous outing. And to top it off, prideful in the thought you bested me, The Devil."

He looked The Devil in the eye ... and smiled. Then he cleared his throat. "And I quote: *'That key will open any lock in existence.'* Those were your exact words.  You also said that there was no time limit, and that I could use it for as long as I wanted."

The Devil shook his head.  "I don't see how that ... wait."  He could see the realization dawning in those beady eyes.

"Any lock," he said.  "Including say ... the Gates of Heaven."

"They'd never let you ..."

"Or, I could use it on the Gates of Hell.  Let all your little buddies out.  I'm sure The Big Guy would get pretty ticked about that."

"You wouldn't!"

"Look in my eyes," The Soldier said.  "Does it look like I won't?"

The Devil considered him for just a moment, then held out his hand.  "Gimme the jacket, bargain unstruck.  We never had any of these conversations.  Never met you before in my life."

He handed the jacket over, but kept the key in his hand.  "This, I'll hold onto.  When I die, you can have it back."

The Soldier pocketed the key, smiling broadly.  "I look forward to never seeing you again, sir."

The Soldier then turned and walked away, and The Devil, sighing heavily, let him go.  He stood there for some time, the collar of the jacket scratching his neck, the early evening mosquitoes buzzing about his head.

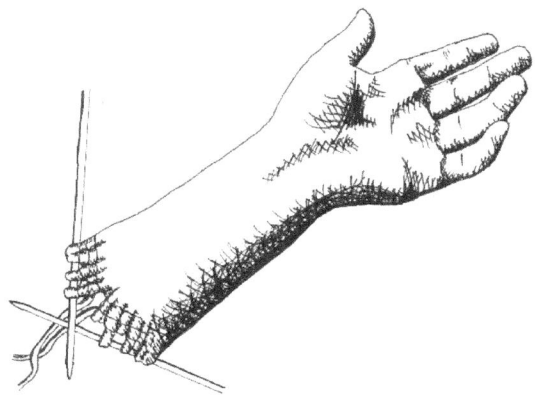

## THUMBLING

by Gregory L. Norris

When news of expecting parents travels word of mouth and secondhand, the usual reaction among family and friends is one of joy, sometimes shock. In the case of Kirsten Daim, the announcement unleashed a curious response: dread.

"Finally, Tom and I will have a family," she said from a corner of the oblong conference table in the bookstore's café.

The whoosh and gurgle of the coffee machines blending and steaming overpriced drinks attempted to drown her voice. The rain hammering the universe beyond the tall panes ratcheted up in intensity. The world outside had been bled of most of its color. The gray seeped in and attempted to devour the deep claret of Ada's yarn. She studied the half-completed scarf and, for a terrible instant, expected it to unravel on its own.

"You're…?" asked Tansy, another of the knitting group's members.

"Pregnant," said Kirsten.

She smiled but even that lacked joy, and seemed more a mischievous grin than an expression of happiness.

Long seconds passed without congratulations. The noise in the café thickened. So did the air. Ada blinked, set down her needles, and rose from the chair, aware of the damp print created by her sweat and the resistance of muscles that didn't want to cooperate.

"Good for you, honey," Ada said. She embraced Kirsten, who hugged back, though stiffly.

"And for Tom. I know how important this is to you both, how hard you've tried."

Trina made an off-color remark—about the hard part and trying. It should have been funny, but none of the women, aged early twenties like Tansy to Ada's still-young fifty-four, laughed.

"Thanks," said Kirsten.

And that was, for the most part, that.

Ada volunteered to buy Kirsten a celebratory drink—providing the mom-to-be could still enjoy caffeinated beverages given her condition. Kirsten assured Ada she could, and then returned to knitting a wooly blanket no bigger than a placemat in a shade of bright butter-yellow that dulled to a sallow jonquil between blinks.

The rain continued to drum against the building as Ada walked back from the café counter with two frozen coffee drinks—French vanilla for Kirsten, a mocha latte for herself. She took one sip and nearly vomited. The milk was sour.

\* \* \* \* \*

Over the next month of weekly meetings, where bored housewives and stressed divorcées gathered to knit, sip overpriced coffee, and chitchat in the café of the big chain bookstore, Ada Godfrey watched Kirsten Daim create articles of clothing of a scale that looked more suited to a doll than a baby. And she wondered if, in fact, Kirsten was pregnant at all or really living out some form of disassociative dream. A kind of fantasy imposed by the mind to save body and soul after two emotionally crippling miscarriages in the same number of years. Doll clothes for a doll that had taken on a life of its own in Kirsten's eyes. The last effort of a damaged psyche trying to protect its owner's sanity.

Kirsten's news lacked the celebratory atmosphere of other birth announcements, and yet Ada attempted to honor the situation with the norm, the expected. The Daims weren't Jewish as far as she knew, so a baby shower didn't need to happen after the actual birth. And though few of the knitting group's members socialized outside of their regular Wednesday night meetings, she figured a shower with cake, coffee, and under-twenty-buck gifts would bring them all closer.

She bought invitations at the Dollar Store—a twelve pack—and golden and purple foil decorations made in China. She knew how to bake and planned on a golden cake with chocolate frosting and cherries on top. Coconut, too, as long as Kirsten wasn't allergic.

Kirsten was twenty-seven, and young mothers, Ada figured, could use all the help possible, so she figured she'd pass the basket for cash for one big group gift.

That next Wednesday, Ada followed Kirsten into the parking lot. A warm end-of-summer night with plenty of stars and a wedge of silver moon hung over the world, the horizon deceptively tranquil.

"Hon," Ada called. "Kirsten?"

Kirsten turned toward the sound of her voice and, for an instant, the image of the mom-to-be filled Ada with revulsion, for her eyes were vacant wells of milky white. Then Ada remembered to breathe and pupils surfaced as she neared.

"A baby shower?"

"Of course—you're one of us."

"Sure," Kirsten said through a saccharine smile. "I'd love that."

Only after that, Kirsten stopped coming to the knitting group, and any attempt to call her cell went directly to voicemail.

She put in twenty bucks from her mad money, collected a hundred and ten from the others, and the sum total went into a pretty card with a cartoon stork on the front. The stork carried a giggling cherub in a cloth hammock—the baby's gender unclear. The only writing on the inside was: *Congratulations on your bundle of joy!*

Autumn approached, and the days grew shorter and darker. The sense of wrongness in the air worsened. Despite Kirsten's continued absence, members of the knitting group stayed home, excusing themselves in emails or phone calls—colds, things to do, deaths in the family, most of which Ada took as white lies.

On that last Wednesday night in late September, wanting to stay home, too, but forcing herself out the door and into her car, Ada found herself sitting alone at the large table in the bookstore's café. No one else showed.

Ada returned home and lit candles—sugar cookie and vanilla, pumpkin spice, and autumn apples—but instead of helping to dispel the gloom, she choked on the fragrances she normally found cheerful. Her little abode on Beecher Road renounced its cozy sense, and contrary to protecting against the looming darkness beyond the new energy efficient windows, it seemed to surrender, and welcomed the wrongness in.

\* \* \* \* \*

A restless wind whistled down from the north. Ada's knitting sat untouched, the same few projects from the summer left unfinished. She'd lost weight though something invisible grew in her gut, like a hysterical pregnancy in response to Kirsten's news from the odd night that now felt ages behind, part of some other life.

That night, Ada realized, was the start of the malaise, the origin of the wrongness. Kirsten's pregnancy, something that should have been cause for celebration, had instead spread misery.

Ada paced the little house. Wind howled around the eaves and sobbed beyond the windows.

She wandered to the desk in the living room, a secretary with cherry veneer, and opened the top right drawer. An address book hid beneath bills. *Kirsten Daim, 112 Winslow Street (Big Green Barn)*.

She debated mailing the card and risking that someone would open it and help themselves to the cash. She could stop at the grocery store less than a mile from her front door and pay a buck-twenty for a money order.

No, Ada thought. The only way to be done with the wrongness was to face it directly. So, at 4:31 p.m. on a windy autumn Tuesday, she picked up the card, grabbed her tote and keys, and drove away from the house where something dark had crept in beneath the windowsills.

\* \* \* \* \*

As the distance lessened, Ada felt the malaise grow, leaving a knot in her stomach and an unpleasant sensation on her tongue akin to the one that comes from licking an envelope or the lingering aftertaste of Diet Anything.

She scanned the Oldies channels on her radio but forgot why she loved those songs, and instead opted to listen to the muffled shouts of the wind. By Winslow Street, a light rain joined in, making the early night even darker.

Turn around, she told herself. Go home and lock the doors, check the windows, extinguish all lights, and pray that whatever was manifested that night in the café, a postpartum spell from a birth as yet unannounced by a young woman perhaps not even with child, passed by, finally disinterested in her.

If Ada did, if she turned back now, she sensed she'd be stuck with the gloom that had gotten under her skin and into her bones.

She drove on.

The barn rose ahead of her, gray in the rain, green only in the car's headlights when Ada turned onto the winding drive. Lights were on in the house. But those seemed twice as far away, hidden behind a filter or film of dark residue. She shut off the engine, reached for her keys, but then thought differently. Keys still in the ignition offered an easier escape if escape was needed. Why she would imagine such a thing troubled her almost as much. The *wrongness* was at its most concentrated. She struggled down her next breath.

Ada stepped out of the car. An earthy mix of wood smoke and damp horse manure reached her through the rain. The bitterness was a welcome anchor, a tangible reminder of the real world. Kirsten loved horses, according to what little Ada knew from her only previous visit. The horse, a fawn-colored female rescue named Butterfly, had been invaluable in keeping its rescuer intact during the chapters of her other, earlier pregnancies.

Another smell drifted among the first, and that one wasn't reassuring. Not in the least. An odor of decaying leaves and dark earth; of carcasses and corpses and spoiled fruit. The gravel driveway and walking path leading up to the front door had absorbed the rain decently, but Ada could see the weedy wildness of the grounds around her. Flowers drooped, and most required deadheading.

Ada realized she stood frozen and was getting soaked. She willed her legs into moving and hurried up the path, to the door. She pressed the doorbell's lit circle, a dim ember. The noise that emerged struck her ears with a sour note, as though sound, too, could somehow decay in the same manner as flesh.

Motion registered behind the drawn curtains and English panes. Ada's pulse quickened. A shape, vaguely human, materialized on the other side of the door, but only seemed half there, a wisp of smoke. The apparition hesitated. Then—

"Who is it?" Kirsten demanded more than asked.

175

"It's me, honey—Ada from the knitting group."

Right as the figure of smoke seemed ready to vanish, the shadow deepened, solidified. A hand unlatched a chain, turned a deadbolt, and the door opened. Kirsten stood on the other side, framed before the backdrop to a charming country-style living room. Plaid, overstuffed sofas and chairs and a brick fireplace hid partially behind her willowy form, her long legs in jeans, her knit top making Ada wonder if she'd continued crafting in private.

"What can I do for you?" Kirsten asked, all business.

The rain spilled down, even worse at the open door because of the gutters.

"Well, for a start, I'd love to get out of this monsoon," Ada said, adding a nervous chuckle that sounded pathetic even to her own ears.

Kirsten glanced to her left and didn't blink. No, maybe she didn't want to enter that house after all, thought Ada. She reached into her bag in search of the card. The envelope eluded her. Ada's eyes drifted back to the door, to Kirsten, who showed no signs of weight gain in what was, according to Ada's math, the mom-to-be's second trimester.

What if she'd lost this baby, too? That would explain the strange malady infecting the days and nights; that postpartum depression hanging thick and sour everywhere one turned.

Ada's fingers brushed a pointed edge. She grabbed hold of the card.

"Of course, come on in," Kirsten said, and welcomed her into the house.

Ada's feet shuffled forward and past the threshold before she could order them to halt. On her way into the house, she noticed Kirsten steal another of those furtive glances leftward. Tom, perhaps? Only Tom wasn't there, just the empty kitchen, and when Kirsten closed the door behind her, the sensation that slithered through Ada's blood was one of being trapped.

"This is a surprise," Kirsten said, and waved her toward the plaid chairs.

Ada sat when she wanted to run. The heat from the fireplace was minimal. A chill pursued her in from the outside. Maybe, Ada thought, the cold was already present and comfortable in the room. "A nice one, I hope."

Again, a second or so passed before Kirsten answered, "Yes," as though all of her responses were on a kind of timed delay. A knot popped in the fireplace. Ada's heart skipped.

"This," she said, and pulled out the envelope. "This is why I'm here, Kirsten. It's a gift from the girls."

She handed the envelope over. The way Kirsten accepted and then opened the card with eyebrows knitted together suggested insult more than a welcomed gift.

"How lovely," Kirsten said. "But you shouldn't have."

"We wanted to do something. You're—"

Kirsten was what? A friend? A colleague if nothing more. One of the knitters. One of the gals.

"You're on all of our minds. We just wanted to be sure that you're all right."

"I'm fine. What makes you think I'm not, Ada?"

"The baby."

"Baby?" Kirsten parroted.

Ada's shoulders shrugged in defiance of the invisible weight pressing down upon them. "Well, I…"

Kirsten stood and glided out of the living room, into the kitchen. "Tea?"

"Sure," said Ada. Anything to be warm again.

Kirsten moved about, out of view. Ada dragged her rump from the plaid chair over to the hearth. The bricks hadn't absorbed the heat from the flames, and radiated a chill through her pants, into her hipbones.

"There is a baby," Kirsten said from the kitchen. "Oh, yes, we created a baby. The tiniest little baby. Tom and I..."

A shiver teased the nape of Ada's neck. She fought it, failed. The room shuddered out of focus around her. When it stabilized, a clink of spoon against cup teased her ears, along with something else—a patter of small footsteps, more those of a mouse behind the walls than anything human. Certainly not Tom's. Baby steps? The tiniest.

"*No*," Kirsten whispered, and Ada knew the hushed command was not for her.

A cat or small dog?

"*Shhh...no.*"

The cold vanished abruptly, driven out by a rush of suffocating heat. Ada stood and shuffled across the floor. A crinkling of packets— surely tea being torn opened for steeping—fought against the drumbeat of her heart. The sound fluttered near Ada's ear, unpleasant like an insect flapping its wings.

Kirsten's back materialized, along with a scene that would appear normal in any other setting: a friend—a colleague—fixing tea. The teakettle gargled. Normal, except—

Ada's eyes fell to Kirsten's right, to the length of counter, attracted by a darting of movement. There, all of the vast wrongness manifested in the guise of a tiny doll, the ugliest she'd ever seen, something barely

178

recognizable as having a human likeness, with mottled flesh and threadbare ginger hair, clad in a green knitted jumper that lent it an amphibian appearance.

The doll sat on the counter, posed with its legs dangling over the edge. *An abomination*, thought Ada. The storm of the past few months...its center, its eye, was mere yards away, wrongness in its purest distillation.

Eye of the storm—and eyes that unleashed a terrible emotion through Ada's insides, across her flesh. That of being watched.

"Kirsten," she said.

Kirsten spun around, her eyes wide. "Yes?"

And then the ugly little doll, which wasn't really a doll, tipped its misshapen head toward Ada and blinked.

In her attempt to reach the car, she fell face down on the ground. Everything after that was painful, with the foul taste of blood and wet earth adding to her panic. For a horrifying instant, Ada didn't know the sky from the ground, up from down. The rules of time, space, and sanity no longer applied. A new order reigned at the Daim farm: Disorder.

Madness.

Ada recovered. The hulking mass of shadows sitting slick in the rain again became her car. She walked her hand along the hood and made it to the door. Keys? *Yes,* she'd left her keys in the ignition. One small facet of sanity prevailed in this new, mad world. But it was short-lived.

She turned the key, and the car rumbled to life. But when Ada tipped a look in the rearview mirror at the long driveway running back to the green barn, the last of her hope suffocated. For blocking her path of escape, at an angle across the driveway, was Kirsten's horse. And sitting upon Butterfly's back without the benefit of saddle was Tom.

### It's a Grimm Life

Ada assumed the rider was Kirsten's husband, whom she'd only met in passing on a few of those lost Wednesday nights that were eons in the past, part of another life and reality. A handsome man, with dirty blond hair kept in a neat, athletic cut and a beard permitted to go wild in contrast. A man's sort of man. He was the perfect match for Kirsten, who was a woman's kind of woman. Perfect, except they were unable to conceive children.

Whatever the identity of the abomination in the kitchen, she was certain it hadn't been birthed by sane or holy methods.

Tom straddled the horse in a rigid, military pose. Ada's foot tapped the brake pedal, and red lights painted Butterfly and Tom, and whatever they were in Ada's thoughts—man and horse—no longer matched with their present state. Vacant eyes glowed the color of blood and turned to glare at her in the rearview mirror.

A blockade.

"Tom, please don't," Ada whimpered.

Some disconnected register still functioning noticed the tiny figure as it scurried down from inside the horse's ear; a thing with spindle limbs and a misshapen representation of a human head clad in a knit jumper— green, Ada guessed, only it came off as black against the red of the taillights.

The abomination slid down the horse's leg, landed on the damp ground, and skittered out of sight. Ada imagined it trotting toward the car. Toward *her*.

She moved her foot from the brake to the gas pedal and gunned it.


\* \* \* \* \*


180

She tasted mud, blood. The echo from the impact reverberated in her ear. Deeper.

Ada attempted to move. The bruises her body had sustained in the collision sent up fresh ribbons of pain and drove away her sluggishness.

"She's awake," said a voice—Kirsten's.

Footsteps pattered; small, bare, *wet* on the floor. Revulsion throbbed through Ada's blood and painted a foul tang in her mouth. The sensation of wrongness drifted around her.

"Don't pretend," another voice hissed into her ear, cold and genderless, *its* voice.

Ada bolted up and kicked away from the tiny creature. In short order, she absorbed her surroundings. She was back inside their house, judging by the furniture—a crib and matching changing table, and framed pictures of teddy bears that should have appeared charming, but worsened the cancer devouring Ada's stomach. This was the room created for children never born.

Several black pillar candles burned atop a dresser and in five points on the floor, forming a pentagram of sorts around her.

"I'm truly sorry, Ada, but we need you," said Kirsten. "We need your essence so that our dear little one can continue to be with us."

Ada scrambled through the candles, toward the door, on tired knees that complained. But something tall and equally ominous blocked the door—Tom. Or what was left of him. She deflected to a corner, where a rocking chair filled the space, along with a basket of bright yarn. The tiny demon hopped over Ada's calf and scrambled up her leg. Even through simple contact, she felt her energy wane. Ada's resistance fizzled. The last foot to the rocker felt more like a gulf of miles.

It stole her energy, fed on her life. Ada remembered how much she'd loved her life, lonely as it was, along with her home, her world.

Her knitting.

She reached into the basket of yarn beside the rocker, where she assumed Kirsten had spent many solemn nights, and found her last desperate hope for escape. Then, as the horror attempted to scale the back of her head, Ada turned, the abomination turned with her, and she drove the knitting needle through its face. A liquid pop sounded as the point of the needle pierced the rear of the horror's skull.

Kirsten screamed. The animated corpse of Tom that blocked the door collapsed. Ada jabbed the needle's point into the wall, scrambled off the floor, and ran from the room, then the house, into the rain-swept night.

FAIRY TALE ENDINGS

by Zoe McAuley

"It's always gladdening to have such kind-hearted people such as yourselves come to visit. It gives us hope—it gives the little ones such hope."

The squat man gave a toothy smile to the couple as he shooed them through yet another beige but subtly stained door. Yet another gloomy corridor snaked out before them, their footsteps crunching on the hairy brown carpet.

"Well, it's hopeful for us, too," said Anna. "We have been thinking about adopting a child for some time."

"Still, still, not many can bring themselves to come to us. Not to our poor darlings. Ah, here we are!" he stopped at a bedroom door indistinguishable for all the others and rapped on it lightly. "Punzy! We've got visitors. May we come in?"

The muffled reply sounded vaguely positive, or at least enough for the small man to decide to open the door.

The little room was freezing. The sash window had been jammed open as high as possible. The curtains had been ripped from their rails and cast on the floor. Tiny snippets of hair clogged the carpet and coated the bedside table.

Most alarmingly, a little girl was perching on the window ledge, her legs propped against the iron cage surrounding the exterior. Her hair was cropped down to an irregular fuzz. She stared down at the street, heedless of the height, gripping a sheet of typed paper tightly in one fist. Anna and John shared a panicked glance, but the master of the orphanage seemed unconcerned.

"Ah Punzy, in your usual spot, I see. Would you care to come in and meet these good people? They might like to be your parents some day."

The girl shook her head fiercely, still staring at the street. He gave an apologetic grin and leaned in close to the couple.

"Poor little Punzy is rather claustrophobic. Raised in rather cramped conditions. But very fond of heights, oddly. The ground appears to alarm her somewhat. Makes day trips difficult. And school. And leaving the building at all, to be honest. Where do you live, by the way?"

"A bungalow in the suburbs," said John. "There's a big open garden ... we thought kids would like that."

"Ah well, often they do, often they do. Perhaps Punzy isn't the child for you, in that case." He raised his voice again. "We'll be going now, Punzy. It was nice to meet you, wasn't it?"

The couple mumbled something to that effect as the door was closed and their guide swept onwards.

184

"Our next little one is more an outdoorsy sort. Well, she used to be, until the unfortunate holiday in the Black Forest. She was lucky that the forest warden got to that cabin when he did, otherwise she might have gone the way of her poor grandmother. Who knew a single wolf could eat so much?"

Another knock, another mumble, another door swung open.

This girl was actually inside her room, sitting in her wheelchair. Lined up on the table next to her were half a dozen knives—the long, sharp knives of a survivalist. She was sharpening another against a whetstone. Her red trousers were folded up at the knees, covering the stumps of her legs, matched by a red baseball cap tugged tightly onto her head.

"Hello, Mr. Grimm," she said calmly.

"Hello, Scarlett. These good people are here to meet you all."

"Hello," she repeated, pausing in her whetting just long enough to glance up at the visitors.

"Those are very ... nice knives you've got there," John said, voice trembling only a little. "I'm surprised you have them here."

"It's best to be prepared," she shrugged. "And I keep them away from the other kids. Mr. Grimm says it's fine as long as I'm careful with them."

Mr. Grimm gave an indulgent smile. "We only want our children to be happy, whatever it takes. John and Anna were just telling me that they live in a bungalow. Wouldn't that be convenient for you?"

Scarlett set aside her knife and gave the guests a proper inspection. She passed over their faces without reaction, but her attention narrowed sharply on John's legs. Her pupils popping wide in terror, she snatched for her knife, levelling it at the guests. Mr. Grimm quickly interposed himself between them.

"Now Scarlett, whatever's gotten into you?"

"On his leg. Hair. There's animal hair. Wolf hairs," she said, the knife quivering in her white-knuckled grasp.

Mr. Grimm turned to the couple. "Have you a dog in this bungalow of yours?"

"Ahh, yes, two, but they're only King Charles spaniels," said Anna. "They're harmless."

"Harmless. Well, yes, harmless. Still, perhaps we should leave poor Scarlett in peace. Good day, my girl."

Mr. Grimm all but shoved them out of the room and slammed the door behind them.

"Should she really have those knives?" John whispered.

"Are you volunteering to take them from her?" Mr. Grimm replied.

In silence, they moved on to another room.

A burst of moist air swirled out with the opening door. Where the other rooms had had desks, this one had a wall of shelves, laden to the point of bowing with vivariums. Unseen things croaked and clicked amidst layers of pebbles, puddles and plants, under sweltering light bulbs. A pale, weedy girl was reaching into one tank to scoop up a squirming tree frog and cradle it in her hands, cooing to it gently.

"Hello there, Lynn, how are the little ones today? Nice and damp?"

She startled at his voice, previously blind to their arrival. Her hands cupped protectively about the little frog.

"Yes, Mr. Grimm. I was just making sure Frederick felt alright after he fell off his favourite twig. He says he's fine, but I think he just wants me to feel better."

"That's very considerate of him. And what about Clarence? You said he was off his flies."

She looked up to another tank, where a fat toad burped serenely on a stone.

"Oh, he's better now. I gave him some of his favourite meal worms and he perked right up."

It was then that Anna's eyes slipped onto a smaller set of tanks. These tanks were crawling with worms or swarming with flies. A few escapees fluttered and writhed upon a slightly crumpled sheet of typed-written paper.

"This is Anna and John, my dear. They're here to meet all the children."

"Hello there, Lynn," Anna tried to throw herself into a chirpy introduction, blocking out the things wriggling all around her. "I see you like pets a lot. I'd love to hear about them."

Lynn scowled. "They're not pets! They're people. People just like the rest of us, but none of you listen. Don't you hear them?"

The little frog in her hands croaked, but it was just a croak. Lynn's shoulders sagged.

"I know, Frederick. Maybe it's not their fault, but they're just so ... so stupid."

Mr. Grimm cleared his throat. "Now Lynn, don't forget you're with guests."

She mumbled something which could conceivably have been "sorry".

"Perhaps we should leave you to your friends," Anna said, edging towards the door.

Mr. Grimm was quick on the hint, and with a barely concealed sigh, brushed them out the door with a curt farewell to Lynn. The girl didn't appear to notice—her attention returned to the frog at once.

"Does she really think those frogs talk?" Anna whispered.

Mr. Grimm shrugged. "Well, can we ever really know the mind of another? But yes, as far as we can tell, she believes that they speak. Poor girl, she isn't even an orphan, but her parents couldn't cope with her anymore. Hit herself in the head with a football and when she came around, she thought frogs were talking to her. She started bringing them home by the bucketful. She says she's trying to find the first one she spoke to—I suspect she was a little enamoured with that one. It all got a bit out of hand really."

They emerged into a lounge, mercifully free of children. Mr. Grimm plopped into a chair and gestured to the couple to do the same.

"Mr. Grimm," Anna said, "these children ... they seem to have some serious issues."

"Well, of course, this is Grimm and Grimm's Home for Tormented Teenagers. We specialise in dealing with the most peculiarly damaged children. If you wanted a convenient child, you should have gone to Andersen's Home for Adorable Angels. I hear those little darlings are very easy to take care of. But our children, well, they're a bit more demanding. But surely helping such troubled children is so much more worthwhile?"

The couple reached for each other's hands.

"I don't think we're up to it," Anna whispered.

With every politeness, Mr. Grimm saw them out of the orphanage and retreated to his office. In the bowels of the old building, the cook yelled for the children to come for their dinner. Mr. Grimm settled at his desk and fed a fresh sheet of paper into his typewriter. He knew it was old-fashioned, but he found that nothing matched the satisfaction of punching the keys and seeing the spindly arms punch the paper.

He wasn't surprised about Anna and John's reaction—from the moment they arrived, it was clear that they weren't made of stern enough stuff, not for his children. Few were. He made the children's lives as comfortable as he could at the home, but the world didn't offer them any happy endings.

Not the real world anyway. He began to stab away at the keys. Today was Scarlett's turn.


*"Once upon a time there was a dear little girl who was loved by everyone who looked upon her, but most of all by her grandmother. The old woman gave her most cherished granddaughter whatever she could, whenever she could. Once, she gave her a little riding hood of red velvet, which suited her so well that she would never wear anything else; so she was always called 'Little Red Riding Hood'."*

## Author Biographies

**Carl Barker** lives and works in the Scottish Borders, where he has been known to occasionally skulk round ruined castles at night, howling at the full moon.

He has published numerous horror short stories over the last few years and is an active member of both The British Fantasy Society and The Horror Writers Association.

You can find him online at www.holeinthepage.co.uk. Be warned though, he bites!

————

**Jessamy Corob Cook** grew up in the English countryside, and spent her time looking for fairies in the woods and fields surrounding the village. She now lives in London, but has not given up on finding fairies. Jessamy is an actress, has also worked as a bookseller, and loves writing stories. Her work is often inspired by fairy tales. She has a BA in Drama and Theatre Studies from the University of Kent.

————

**Liz Crossland** is a writer, linguist, and educator with a passion for Yorkshire tea. She is fascinated by the structure of languages and has a degree in English Language and Linguistics from Durham University as well as an MA in Professional Writing from Falmouth University.

Her work has been featured in the anthology *Casting Shadows: Extraordinary Tales from New Writers*. She is currently writing a novel about speed-date rambling and malevolent sheep. When she is not writing, Liz enjoys climbing and Ceroc dancing (but not at the same time). She has lived in many countries including Italy, Poland, and Cornwall.

————

Born and raised in Australia, **E. M. Eastick** worked as an environmental professional in Britain, Ireland and the Middle East before turning her hand to writing. Her creative efforts appear or are forthcoming in a number of online and printed publications including the ***Journal of Compressed Creative Arts***, *Skipping Stones Magazine*, and *Mad Scientist Journal*. She currently lives in Colorado.

————

Books claimed **Victor Hyde** at the age of six and since then he has been working hard to make a contribution of his own to the literary world. Bred in South Africa, Victor has experienced both the beauty and terror offered by the dark continent and works to portray this in his work. When not reading and writing, Victor fights to regain control of his house from his wife and two cats.

————

**Steve Keteltas** is a retired computer professional and part-time teacher who now enjoys life as a poet and musician in Seminole, FL. He is a proud member of Pinellas Authors and Writers Organization and has a penchant for twisting words.

————

**T. S. Kummelman** is a 45-year-old single dad living in Odessa, FL. He has two teenagers, so evil fairy tales are right up his alley. He is a contributing writer for Tactitus Publishing, and in his free time practices being sarcastic. His day job involves a cubicle, a phone, and florescent lighting.

————

**Charie D. La Marr** is primarily known as a ghostwriter in the field of sports - mostly baseball. She has had at least one book go to #1 on Amazon in its category.

Currently working to establish herself as an author in her own name, she has created a genre called Circuspunk (listed at Urban Dictionary) and written a collection of short stories in the genre called *Bumping Noses and Cherry Pie*. She is known for writing in many different genres from crime to bizarro to erotica and even Seussian. She is most proud of working with an Iranian translator, translating Booker Man Award Winner *Vernon God Little* into Persian—which became a bestseller in Iran.

A redhead with a redheaded attitude, she lives in NY with her mother and son and fur children Bailey Corwin, Babe Ruth and Casey Stengel.

———————

**Zoe McAuley** grew up near Belfast, but now lives in the north of England. She spent several years studying archaeology at Durham University and is now very good at staring at old walls. These days she sells toy weapons for grown-ups and writes speculative fiction.

———————

**Adrean Messmer** lives in Oklahoma with a tiny human she created from some spare parts and her technowizard husband. She is a member of the Horror Writers Association and the Oklahoma Writing Federation. Her main goal in life is to give others as many awesome nightmares as she has.

———————

**Gregory L. Norris** writes full time from the outer limits of New Hampshire. His work appears regularly in national magazines and fiction anthologies, and he has written for both TV and film. Norris is devoting 2015 -- his fiftieth year on Spaceship Earth -- to completing many of the unwritten tales in his idea catalog that howl at him in the night for their THE ENDs.

———————

**Brett Parker** spends his days working in a refinery, mistrusting felines, and getting pleasure from fixing things of a mechanical nature. He is also known in certain circles as having an excellent collection of ball caps.

————

**Richard Tasonmart** lives and works on a mountain overlooking a lake in Snowdonia National Park in Wales. This is his first published short story, although it won't be his last. He sometimes tweets at @rtasonmart.

————

**Carmen Tudor** writes from Melbourne, Australia. Catch her latest spec fic in *Fantasy For Good*, *Tales of Mystery, Suspense & Terror*, and *Magical: An Anthology of Fantasy, Fairy Tales, and Other Magical Fiction*. You can follow Carmen's tweets under @carmen_tudor or check her out at carmentudor.net.